The Lady and the Duke

Robyn C Rye

Published by robyncrye, 2022.

Also by Robyn C Rye

Farnsworth Sisters
Marrying a Rogue
Rescuing Hannah

The Buckingham Sisters
Lady Maggie's Challenge
Layla's Unwanted Husband

The Evans Family
Sometimes Love is not Enough
Still the One
Moving Forward

Standalone
One More Chance
Lady Jayne's Reputation
Third Time's the Charm
Can't Stop Loving You

The Marriage Scam
An Unlikely Match
Searching For You
The Unexpected Suitor
The Lady and the Duke
Starting Over
An Unforgettable Stranger
The Duke's Revenge
The Temporary Wife
Against The Odds
Betrayed
No Good Turn Goes Unpunished
Lady Eloise's Soldier
Lillian's Forbidden Beau
Remember Me
Always Second Best
When One Door Closes
Coming Home to You
Chasing Shadows
Fool Me Once
Deserting Lady Audrey
My Unlikely Saviour
Lies and Deception
A New Beginning
Julia's Second Chance
The Hidden Enemy
The Maiden's Redemption
Miss Elizabeth's Season

Table of Contents

Chapter One 1

Chapter Two 7

Chapter Three 11

Chapter Four 15

Chapter Five 20

Chapter Six 25

Chapter Seven 33

Chapter Eight 41

Chapter Nine 46

Chapter Ten 54

Chapter Eleven 61

Chapter Twelve 66

Chapter Thirteen 73

Chapter Fourteen 80

Chapter Fifteen 84

Epilogue 93

Copyright © 2020 by Robyn C Rye

Author's Message

Thank you for joining me in telling the story of Olivia and Charles. I hope you enjoyed their story as much as I enjoyed recounting it.

If you enjoyed the book and have a moment to spare, I would appreciate a brief review on the page or site where you purchased the book. Your help in spreading the word is appreciated. Reviews from readers like you make a massive difference in helping new readers find stories like *The Lady and the Duke.*

Thank you!

Robyn C Rye

robyncrye.author@gmail.com

Chapter One

Charles

While Charles dressed for the evening, he considered staying in, but having made arrangements with his friends, it would be bad manners not to arrive. In need of a drink, Charles settled in his favourite chair in the library and closed his eyes. A tap on the door drew his eyes to his butler, who hovered in the doorway.

"My lord, Jenkins wondered if you wanted the carriage tonight?"

"Yes, I should go, although I'd prefer a night at home. I think I am getting too old for this endless stream of social events, drinking and gambling. It might be time to consider returning to the country."

When Charles called for his carriage, he did so with resignation. He was to meet his cohort of friends at one of the city's most prestigious gaming hells, where they would drink too much, gamble recklessly and end the night with a light skirt in their arms. His disinterest tonight in his usual distractions was a feeling that had been growing for weeks. Indeed, there must be more to life than endless nights spent with other wastrel sons of the ton. When his father released him from estate duties, neither expected Charles to leave his home for years. His father was getting on in years; perhaps it was time to return home, allowing his father to retire from the rigorous duties that came with being a duke.

The carriage pulled up outside the establishment that was well-known to the gamblers of the ton. The outside of the building resembled a family home, but inside, there was nothing homely about the décor. Charles weaved through crowds of revellers, some already in their cups at this early hour. His friends and acquaintances had already appropriated a table where a card game was underway, and his arrival prompted greetings from some of the players. At the same time, others' concentration stayed firmly on the cards in front of them, suggesting the severe nature of the bets already placed. Sliding into a seat next to his oldest friend, Hamilton Brewer, the earl of Cloverly, Charles shook his head at the suggestion they let him in when this game ended.

It was hard for Charles to identify his discontent, but he couldn't gather any enthusiasm for the endless pursuits that generally held him in thrall. When female arms wrapped around his neck, the perfume his admirer wore engulfed him, and he felt an urgent need to push her away so that he could breathe. Fighting the urge to shove the woman, Charles unwound the arms as gently as possible and moved away from the woman. She raised her eyebrows at him, and he shook his head.

"Sorry, Sienna, I'm not in the mood tonight."

The woman smiled coquettishly and tapped him with her fan.

"I'm sure I can put you in the mood."

"Damn it, woman, I said no!"

Charles sighed; he hadn't meant to snap at the woman, but the arms around his neck and the blatant offer made him feel suffocated. As the offended woman stalked away, Hamilton raised his eyebrows.

"Not in the mood? Are you ill? I've never seen you turn down a woman's offer before."

Charles shrugged."There's a first time for everything."

Hamilton slapped him on the back. "Let's get a few drinks into you and see how you feel then."

Charles groaned as he rolled over. His head pounded, and his eyes ached; if he didn't know that his afflictions resulted from over-imbibing the night before, he might have convinced himself that he had a deadly disease. Charles fought off nausea with his eyes fixed on the ceiling and slightly elevated his head. Damnation; why did he put himself through this agony every morning? He and his friends neglected their duties and ran riot amongst the ladies of the ton, drinking too much and gambling away their heritage. Waking with a hangover was getting old, and Charles decided that this morning was the last he would wake feeling like death. Tomorrow, he would turn over a new leaf.

His resolution did nothing to help with the hangover currently causing him misery. Charles's mind drifted back over the years. For years, Charles had known that when his father died, he would assume the duties of his estates and unentailed properties. His future was something he accepted, and he fulfilled all the obligations of a boy and then, as a young man, those his father required. When his boyhood friend headed off to the Peninsula to fight alongside Lord Hamilton, Charles remained at home because, as the only Duprais family heir, his father did not wish to have his son and heir injured or killed.

Confined to the estate, Charles fought against the restrictions placed on him. He was not involved in running the estates, and his father was fit and healthy and destined to live for another twenty or thirty years, so he felt useless and bored. Understanding his son's frustration, Lord Henry Duprais gave his son leave to attend social events and mix with young men of the ton. That was ten years ago, and although Charles checked on his father occasionally, he rarely spent time on the estate with his father.

A knock on the door dragged him from his reminiscing, and his valet entered the room. Walters had been a fixture in Charles's life since his father deemed him old enough to have a servant of his own, and he was the one person Charles could bear to see this early in the day. As usual, Walters carried a jug of tea and a large cup this morning. Walters swore the tea was therapeutic, but Charles never felt better, even after drinking gallons of it.

"Why do I subject myself to this misery every morning, Walters?"

"I'm sure I don't know, my lord. It's not as if the cause of your misery isn't well known to you. I'll draw you a bath, which might help you feel better."

A knock on the door startled both Walters and Charles. Who would need to speak to him before breakfast? Walters opened the door to find the butler standing on the threshold with a letter in his hand.

"My apologies, my lord, but this letter was delivered, and the messenger said it was a crucial matter you needed to address urgently."

Charles rolled out of bed and groaned as he stood. The sender had folded the letter neatly, but no crest or sender's name was on the outside. Conscious of the sender's desire for Charles to address the problem urgently, Charles opened the letter. It took only the first few lines for him to decipher the message. His father was ill, and the sender, the steward at his father's estate, had written to notify Charles. The steward, Bentley, felt that his father's condition had deteriorated recently, and he thought that Henry Duprais had only a short time to live. He urged Charles to make haste and visit his father.

With the steward's warning ringing in his ears, Charles dressed, and while Walters packed a trunk, he organised the coach to leave within the hour. Charles tasked the butler with closing the townhouse, and he, the housekeeper and the cook would accompany his valet to the estate when they had completed the job.

Guilt was Charles's companion as he cantered along the roads and laneways leading to his home. The journey took two days in a coach to reach the Duprais manor house, but Charles did not have enough patience to sit hour upon hour in the carriage, drawing slowly closer to his destination. He could make the estate in little more than a day if he changed horses at the Faraday Inn, which he decided to do. The last time he spoke to his father was weeks and weeks ago. Had his illness come on quickly, or was his father trying to spare him the grief of watching him die? What if Bentley hadn't sent a message? The thought that his subsequent communication from the estate telling him his father was dead didn't bear considering.

As he neared the estate, Charles felt both anxious and angry. Why had it taken so long for someone to notify him that his father was dying?

Why hadn't he thought to visit his father to check on his welfare? With regret, Charles slid from the saddle and noticed the sweat coating the horse's body and its heaving breaths. He handed the tired horse to the groom, who ran to meet him, and he strode towards the door, which opened at his approach. Graves, his father's butler and a stalwart of the manor, greeted Charles.

"Welcome, my lord. Do you wish to freshen up, or would you prefer to see your father immediately?"

"Graves, I will see my father now, but I want to know why no one notified me about my father's illness sooner?"

"My lord, we tried to convince the duke that you would want to spend time with him, but he said you would have enough to deal with when he was gone, so he didn't intend to burden you with his ill health."

Charles shook his head and walked toward his father's study. The sight that greeted him made him wince; his father was a shadow of his former self. The duke's clothes hung off his frail frame, and his skin's grey pallor didn't bode well for the future.

"Charles, my son, this visit is a nice surprise."

"Damn you, father. Why wasn't I notified of your illness sooner? How can you believe I would be content drinking and gambling in the city while you lie abed with a serious illness?"

"Ah, from your comment, I assume someone ignored my instructions not to tell you."

"Yes, Bentley sent a message that I received yesterday, and for that kindness, I intend to increase his wage."

"Sit down, son; now that you are here, we have some things to discuss."

"Let me ask Graves to organise a plate of cold cuts or some bread and cheese. I am famished as I only stopped to change horses, so I haven't eaten."

Charles and his father chatted, discussing estate matters and finally touching on the duke's illness.

"The doctor says I will grow weaker, and he expects that I will pass away within weeks. I have tried to give you freedom over the past decade, but soon, it will be time for you to take over the estate and the unentailed properties. Please find a wife, not a flashy debutant, but someone you like and who can help you build a family. I loved your mother, and I want that for you, too. A family is the greatest joy a man can have. Your mother and I were only blessed with you, but I hope that the right woman can be the mother to your children. Promise me you will give up your wild lifestyle and find a wife."

It tore at Charles's heart to hear his father speak of his imminent death, but the least he could do was promise the man the one thing that could make him go to his maker, content that his beloved estate would remain in the family.

Chapter Two

Six Weeks Later

The staff and other mourners departed, leaving Charles alone at his father's gravesite. The grey sky reflected Charles's mood, and despite the condolences of the other mourners, Charles felt miserable. He cursed himself for wasting time with dissolute nobles when he should have been here with his father. His father's health had failed so quickly that he faded day by day once Charles had returned home. His world had changed, and he had the duties of a duke to take up, as well as the promise to his father to find a wife. With a sigh, Charles gave one more sorrowful look at his father's grave and walked away to meet the solicitor for the reading of the will. Charles expected there to be no surprises in his father's last will, and other than bequests to the staff, everything his father owned would become his property.

Charles sat in a chair in the library, surrounded by his late father's staff. Once the solicitor read the endowments for the staff, they would return to their duties, and the man would acknowledge the remaining inheritance to Charles. The solicitor droned on, listing gifts for the servants who had served the duke well during his life and then moved on to the estate and unentailed properties. Reading through the list of properties and investments that Charles was to inherit was unnecessary. As the only heir, everything the duke owned went to his son, so this reading wasted time. Once Chatterley, the solicitor, finished reading the will, he shook Charles's hand, repeated his condolences, and departed.

Alone in the house, Charles felt grief and regret overwhelm him. His father had allowed him to socialise and mix with the ton's elite, and Charles regretted becoming so self-indulgent that it never occurred to him to return and ease his father's burden. Regrets could never erase his thoughtlessness, so Charles had to move forward and fulfil his father's last request. Finding a woman whom he wanted to marry was a problem in itself. A giggly debutant or a simpering miss would drive him to drink, but surely, there must be one woman in town whom he could bear.

After reading the will, Charles knew that he had to return to the city to find a bride, so for now, he would close the Manor house. The staff had spent the last few weeks preparing the house for closure. The staff had covered the furniture with dust sheets, cleaned the hearths, and given the remaining food to the tenant farmers. He sent the staff to spend time with their families after the funeral and headed back to London to fulfil his father's last wish.

When Charles closed the door to the manor house, he wondered how soon he would return with a bride. He had to honour his father's wish to marry, but a giggling, blushing debutant was not on his agenda. Were there level-headed debutantes looking for a husband? He wanted a woman who saw his worth, not his title and wealth. Did such a woman exist? How many events would he have to attend before he found a woman he could stand to live with?

Charles cast aside his disreputable friends, save for Hamilton. Hamilton laughed at the suggestion when Charles told his friend he needed to find a bride, but sobered when Charles explained that it was his father's last wish. The gentlemen took up residence in the ducal townhouse, and Charles used his father's man of business to hire workers for the sparsely staffed property.

Before choosing a bride, the difficult task was to convince the society matrons that he had reformed and was worthy of consideration. The two gentlemen walked in the park at the communal times, tipping their hats at people they recognised. Some mornings, they rode early, keeping their horses to a sedate walk or trot. Charles felt grateful that his friend accompanied him on most of his outings, but after three weeks of impeccable behaviour, he became frustrated at the lack of invitations. When he expressed his concern, Hamilton chuckled.

"Whoever thought you'd rue the lack of invitations? You are a duke, and I am an earl. Why not ask the hostesses to include us on their invitation lists? If they decline, we'll turn up; it's not as if they'd throw us out."

Charles sat at his desk, penning notes to the ladies of the ton, citing his reformation and desire for a bride. Once the footmen delivered the messages, the two friends could do little more than wait and hope for the best. When the invitations began to trickle in, Charles heaved a sigh of relief.

Night after night, Charles and Hamilton dressed in their finest clothes and joined the ton at balls and soirees while scouting the debutants for a likely bride. At the beginning of his search, Charles danced with many different girls, only to discover that the virginal debutants could not converse about topics other than fashion. He would scream if he had to give another opinion on the ribbon colour his dancing partner chose to accessorise their outfit.

As the season progressed, the society matrons became aware of Charles's previous behaviour and reputation. The debutant mommas decided he was too risky to allow their daughters to associate with; simply dancing with the man could ruin their marriage prospects. Even though he had little interaction with eligible brides, the invitations continued to arrive.

"Why did I think I could find a bride amongst these innocents? How am I to fulfil my father's final wish?"

"I have a suggestion as a last resort. Cast your eye over the wallflowers, choose the best option and compromise her."

"Damnation, it might come to that. But even if I stoop to that level, it doesn't assure me I will find somebody with some intelligence. The thought of meeting any of those ninnies every morning over the breakfast table doesn't fill me with delight. I thought my title and wealth would be a lure, but even that is not enough to convince these damn mothers to let me converse with their daughter. They rush away when I approach as though I am contagious."

Hamilton patted him consolingly on the arm.

"You promised your father you would marry, but he didn't set a deadline. He wouldn't want you to marry an unsuitable deb to fulfil his last wish."

Charles nodded. His friend was correct; there was no deadline to meet.

Chapter Three

Olivia

Olivia crested the rise and gazed out at the lush green fields below. She felt a sense of sadness, knowing that soon she would be whisked off to London to begin the season, and her opportunities to ride would be limited to leisurely walks in manicured parks. While Olivia's sister was excited about their upcoming trip, Olivia could barely raise any interest. At eighteen, Olivia had no desire to become the property of some man, and she knew that her father might decide on her future husband unless she could convince him she was actively looking for a spouse. With a sigh, she turned her horse and headed for home.

A carriage pulled up to the front of the house, roused her curiosity, but not enough to give it more than a fleeting glance. Perhaps the visitor was an acquaintance of her father who called to discuss last-minute business before their departure. With a shrug, she entered the house.

The number of trunks stacked against the walls impeded her movement when she entered the foyer. Olivia wondered if the maids had left enough garments for the days before their departure or if she would have to send the maid downstairs to search the luggage for clothes. Good grief, did they need to take every item of clothing they owned? She had nearly escaped the madness in the foyer when her mother caught up with her.

"Goodness, Olivia, you're never where you are supposed to be. The Lord Chamberlain has called to speak with your father, and he hopes to pay his respects to you. Run upstairs quickly and get cleaned up. Don't dally; the man won't wait all day."

Now that Olivia knew who the visitor was, she regretted returning to the house before nightfall. God forbid if this man had thoughts of offering for her. The man was old enough to be her father, and, with a potbelly and aggressive nature, he was the last man she would accept if he offered for her. Chamberlain was a widower, having lost his young wife some twelve months ago, and now that his mourning period was over, he could look for a replacement wife without being criticised by society. Why the man thought she was an option was a mystery to Olivia, but she did as her Mother instructed and tidied herself for the visitor. She smoothed her hair and slipped out of her riding habit into the dress on the bed. Lady Clayborne must have instructed her maid about how Olivia needed to present herself so she could find an appropriate garment. Damn her parents! Why would they think the horrid man would make a good match for their daughter?

Grayson opened the door for Olivia, and she grimaced at him; his expression was sympathetic. Olivia felt happier that she had at least one person in the household who recognised her reluctance to speak with the man. Olivia entered, and Chamberlain walked towards her with hands outstretched as though he intended to greet her with a hug. Olivia stepped back quickly, and the man frowned but dropped his hands.

"Come, Olivia, there is no need to be standoffish. If I can't greet the daughter of my great friend Edward, there must be something wrong with the rules of etiquette."

"You may be a great friend of my father, but we are barely acquainted. Society would be shocked if my fiancé greeted me with open arms, so greeting a casual acquaintance with a hug would ruin my reputation."

Olivia chose a single-seated chair, and Lord Chamberlain had no option but to sit across the room. Where on earth had her mother disappeared? Didn't she need a chaperone? Olivia jumped from her chair and headed towards the door. When she pulled the door open, Grayson appeared.

"Can I be of assistance, Miss Olivia?"

"Where is my mother? I need a chaperone, and she has disappeared."

Grayson's face showed no expression, but his eyes held a wealth of understanding.

"Your mother said she had important business to conduct and would return later."

Olivia remained in the open doorway as she stared at the man seated in his chair.

"Come, come, Olivia, we don't need a chaperone. Your mother has given us privacy so I can ask you an important question. Come inside and close the door."

"Grayson, please leave the door open and ask Pearl to join me. I am amazed that my mother suddenly thinks I don't need a chaperone. I'm not foolish enough to be caught in a room with a man, whoever he may be."

Olivia walked into the room and stood on the other side of Chamberlain. The man rose and moved towards her, and Olivia backed away. She heard him huff, and then he said, "I have spoken to your father, and he has permitted me to ask you if you would give me leave to court you. You will not need to go to London for your season because I will offer it to you after an appropriate time."

Olivia backed away from the man, her face pale and tears welling. With Grayson standing at the door, she moved to the entrance.

"Lord Chamberlain, I am honoured that you want to court me, but I must decline. I intend to have my season in London with my sister."

She stepped out of the room and past Grayson.

"What is wrong with my parents if they think that man is a good match for me? He is fat, old, and has a nasty temper. He probably beat his last wife to death. I'd rather marry a pauper than marry that man."

As she finished her rant, her mother approached her.

"What is going on here, Olivia? I thought Lord Chamberlain wanted to tell you that your father has permitted him to court you."

"So you left me alone with him so he could compromise me, and then I would have no alternative but to marry the horrid man. I don't know how my father could think to marry me off to that violent leecher. I don't care what the men have agreed upon, but this is my life, and I will not imprison myself in a relationship to satisfy my parents. I would appreciate it if you wouldn't put me in that situation again. Were you going to return, open the door and accuse Lord Chamberlain of ruining me so we would have to marry? What a nasty trick from someone who is supposed to care for me."

Lady Clayborne had the decency to blush before blustering a reply.

"Goodness, Olivia, you do go on. What did you tell Lord Chamberlain?"

"I told Chamberlain that I didn't agree to him courting me and that I was to have a season in London."

Lady Clayborne sighed. "Your father and I thought it would be a good match because we knew you weren't thrilled about travelling to London. If you marry Lord Chamberlain, you can stay in the country, which is all you've ever said you want to do."

"So, under the guise of looking after me, you would marry me off to the most despicable man I know. He has nothing to recommend himself. He is old, fat, lecherous, and has a bad temper. Rumour has it his last wife went gratefully to meet her maker. I don't understand why he and Father are great friends, but be that as it may, he is not the man for me. Before you agree to a man you think of as a good match for me, close your eyes and imagine that man naked, touching you; if you shudder in disgust, he is not the man for me. I will go to London with a smile and chat and dance with every young man I meet rather than tying myself to a man of that ilk."

"Goodness, Olivia, you say the most outrageous things. If you continue to be outspoken, it wouldn't surprise me if you remained a spinster."

"Well, at least that will be my choice."

Chapter Four

The journey to London seemed endless. Thankfully, her father had taken overnight accommodation at two well-respected inns, so they were refreshed and eager to see the city this morning. Olivia and Georgia goggled at the scene from their window seat as the Clayborne carriage rattled through the city streets. The noise from hundreds of thousands of people stunned the girls, and the stench that permeated the air made Olivia reach for her handkerchief to cover her nose. The people congregating on the streets were ragged and poorly dressed, and Olivia felt awkward flaunting their wealth in front of so many poor people. Tears welled when an urchin ran alongside the coach, begging for pennies. Left to her, Olivia would have emptied her reticule into the boy's open hands, but her father put out his hand as she opened the purse.

"You can't help them all, Olivia, so keep your purse closed. It might make you feel better to hand out money, but you will make us a target for many more people to beg at our windows. We will be through this part of the town soon, and then you won't have to see how others live."

Olivia shook her head. How could she socialise and eat well when so many others had so little? She knew what her father said about not helping everyone, but did the people here choose to live in poverty, or did circumstances force them to live amongst the busy, filthy streets? Her father's comment about leaving this part of the city soon became a reality, and Georgia and Olivia exclaimed at the grand houses and the vast, clean streets. Fashionably dressed women walked along, escorted by well-dressed gentlemen. Was this how she would spend her time in the city, parading around for others to see? When she thought back to Lord Chamberlain's proposal, she admitted that she would much rather be here to be seen and socialise than at home being courted by the elderly widower.

The carriage stopped at the front of a two-storey building. Large pillars adorned the front of the house, and elaborate gardens extended from the side of the building, running the entire length of the structure. Olivia was curious to investigate the walled-garden area, but first, she had to explore this house that was to be home for the season ahead.

Lord Clayborne alighted from the carriage and helped his wife and daughters disembark. When the door opened, Olivia smiled at the stern face of the butler. Despite the treatment the rest of the family gave the servants, Olivia took the time to get to know them and treat them as equals, not just helpers. Georgia couldn't understand her sister's actions but shrugged when Olivia spoke about the staff as if they were anything other than servants. A flurry of retainers collected trunks and carried them to their destinations while the housekeeper introduced herself to Lord and Lady Clayborne. The girls were eager to see their rooms, but Lady Clayborne asked for a light lunch, which the family would eat in the breakfast room, and then she would allow the girls to see their rooms.

When the food arrived, Lord Clayborne filled a plate and left the room to ensconce himself in the study. This room would be his bolt-hole for the season, and he would only attend the first social events with his family. He understood the season's importance but left the choice of social activities and the chaperoning to his wife. When Lady Clayborne and the girls finished their meal, their mother left them to settle into their bedrooms.

"We will stroll in an hour or two, so be sure to change your gowns and get Patsy to arrange your hair."

The girls disappeared to explore their rooms, aware that they would feel the wrath of their mother should they arrive late for the walk. Here, a walk was not for enjoyment or exercise but for people to see them. It amused Olivia that she rode for pleasure at home, not requiring an audience to make the activity worthwhile. She wondered if the house they had rented for the season came equipped with horses; it was a question she intended to ask their father at dinner time.

Preparing for a stroll was not a small undertaking. Once attired in the right outfit, the strollers required hats, parasols, and a footman to accompany the women. Lady Clayborne mapped out a route that passed the most prestigious houses, all the better to announce their arrival. If luck was with them, the women might encounter new acquaintances, making their entry into social activities easier.

Olivia loathed the polite chit-chat that ensued. Who cared about where you bought the lovely ribbon adorning your hair or how tiresome it was to purchase new slippers continually? Mindful of the alternative to attending the season, she plastered on a fake smile and made appropriate agreeing noises. She contained her sigh of relief when the ladies they had met moved on, and her mother deemed the excursion a success; they headed for home. Once they arrived home, Olivia wanted to curl up in the library with a book. Still, Lady Clayborne demanded her presence as she and Georgia looked through the invitations that had arrived even before their arrival. Choosing the right invitations was a skill every young woman should learn, according to their Mother.

The first social activity the family attended was at Countess Merryman's home. Invitations to the garden party were in great demand, and Lady Clayborne considered herself lucky that the countess had invited them. She put their invitation down to curiosity and their good showing when they met the ladies on their walk. People mingled; many were already acquainted, and the newcomers easily joined the group.

The protocol in meeting gentlemen was for an acquaintance or friend of another to offer the introductions, but if adhered to for newcomers, no openings could occur. Olivia and Georgia were unknown to the gentlemen attending the gathering, so a few bold souls introduced themselves to Lady Clayborne. A short conversation ensued, in which time their mother would decide on the worth of the gentlemen and then present them to her daughters. One of the gentlemen her mother introduced to Georgia and Olivia reminded her of Lord Chamberlain, and she vowed to keep her distance from the man. Why didn't her mother see the man under the smooth clothes without the title? There was more to life than marrying a man with a title when he repulsed you, and this man, Lord Collingwood, was certainly repulsive. His immediate attention to Olivia made her squirm, and she vowed she would not encourage his interest; however, her mother did nothing to aid her endeavour. When Lord Collingwood asked Olivia to stroll in the garden with him, her mother gave her approval with a smile. The satisfied expression changed when Olivia rejected Lord Collingwood's suggestion.

"Lord Collingwood, while I am flattered that you asked me to stroll in the gardens, as this is the first event I have attended, I feel it is unwise to show interest in a man I have just met. The season is long, and I wish to enjoy the socials and balls without being indebted to any particular gentleman. I'm sure you understand."

When the disgruntled man walked away, Lady Clayborne tutted at Olivia.

"The man is an earl, Olivia. You could do a lot worse."

"Mother, you make me want to scream. Do you not look past the title to the man behind the superficial front? That man will cause me problems at other events, and you have encouraged him by smiling benignly at him. If you sell me off to the first gentleman who shows an interest, I might as well have stayed at home and married the despicable Lord Chamberlain. Why do you insist I should settle for some fat, repulsive man when you don't pressure Georgia? She is older than me; shouldn't she have first call on the old fat men you deem suitable? I want a man with integrity, someone I can grow fond of over the years.

A title doesn't ensure a happy marriage and doesn't ensure that the man is a gentleman. I want to be happy with the man I commit my life to."

Chapter Five

Olivia ran nervous hands along the side of her dress.

"Don't fidget, Olivia," her mother hissed.

Olivia removed her hands and demurely placed them in front of her. Georgia, her older sister, smiled at her. Standing in the receiving line was tedious, but if one wanted others to acknowledge you, it was necessary. The loud monotone of the presenter announced. "Lord Edward Clayborne, Earl of Shropshire, Lady Clayborne, Lady Georgia and Miss Olivia."

A series of bows and curtsies occurred as the group moved along the receiving line. Once free of the crowd, Edward headed straight for the card room. While he accepted his duty to accompany his family, he had no intention of participating in polite chitchat and gossip.

Lady Clayborne ushered her daughters further into the ballroom. She hoped her daughters could catch the eye of the noblemen in attendance. Soon, the gentlemen presented themselves for introductions to both girls. They were both attractive and had decent-sized dowries, so men were always willing to dance and socialise with the ladies. Happy that she had done her job, Lady Clayborne retired to find her cronies.

When Lord Brunswick approached Georgia with a smile and a dashing bow, Olivia realised that the man sought out Georgia every time they attended a function. He had the required title, was tall and well-built and appeared to dote on Georgia. Something about the man raised her suspicions, but she found it difficult to pinpoint his fault. She gave a mental shrug. The man's attention flattered Georgia, so who was she to disagree?

Both sisters joined the first set of dances, and when a brief break in the music occurred, Olivia left the dance floor. Georgia had partners for the following sets, but Olivia had spare places on her dance card. Other ladies without partners congregated together and viewed the proceedings. A tap on her shoulder caused her to turn, and it took all her self-control not to grimace.

"Miss Olivia, it's come to my attention that you have vacancies on your dance card. Either that or a cad has left you in the lurch. May I have your card to write my name in two places?"

The rule of society was that debutantes must accept each invitation to dance. Olivia was desperate to disallow the man the opportunity to dance with her, but respectful manners prevailed. Once Lord Collingwood wrote his name, he smiled at her. The smile was more of a leer, and his eyes never made it past her bodice.

"I will return in due time. I look forward to spending supper time with you."

Olivia's mood dimmed. Goodness, first she had to deal with Chamberlain, and now she had to suffer Lord Collingwood. Why did she attract lecherous old me? A comment from her friend, Lady Agnes, didn't help her disposition.

"Gosh, I'm glad that slimy toad didn't ask me to dance. Did you notice that the man never looks his partner in the eyes?"

"Yes, and he sweats. What am I to discuss during supper? I guess it won't matter if all he intends to do is leer at my bosoms."

Too soon, Lord Collingwood arrived to escort Olivia onto the dance floor. It dismayed her when she realised that the dance was a waltz. Lord Collingwood pulled her into his embrace. Olivia struggled in his grip.

"Please, Lord Collingwood, you are holding me too tightly. We are too close for respectability, and the gossips will talk."

Lord Collingwood did not release her but continued with the dance. Olivia could see fans fluttering as the matrons glared at her and her partner. When the dance finished, she stepped away from her partner.

"Excuse me, my lord, I must visit the lady's retiring room."

"But supper is being served. You need to go with me to the refreshment room."

"My apologies," Olivia said as she dashed towards the retiring room. In the privacy of the room, Olivia shuddered. She moved to a basin of water and washed her hands. Even with gloves on, Olivia could feel the man's sweaty palms and the damp patch on her dress where his hand had rested. How long could she stay here? With one more dance with him on her card, she wasn't in any hurry to return to the ballroom. Olivia looked around; she was alone. The other ladies would be eating supper with their partners, and she was hiding here.

The door opened, and Lady Clayborne and two other matrons entered. Her mother gaped and said,

"Olivia, goodness! What are you doing lurking in here? You are missing out on supper."

"That is the reason I am here. I have no intention of returning until the guests have finished eating."

"Didn't I see you dancing with Lord Collingwood before supper? Doesn't he expect you to join him?"

Olivia shuddered. "The man will only realise I am absent because he will have to leer at other unfortunate ladies."

"Olivia! What the dickens has gotten into you?"

"Mother, ladies, before judging my poor behaviour, ask any other ladies in the ballroom. He holds us too close, leers at our bosoms, and sweats all over us. Touch the back of my dress and explain why I must return for the rest of the tea break."

"Do I need to point out that the man is a gentleman with a title? You cannot ignore him."

"Mother, a title does not make the man a gentleman. I have an idea. I will explain to Lord Collingwood that I am unwell and unable to dance again tonight. You, mother, will take my place as his dance partner. After the dance, you can tell me about his gentlemanly behaviour."

The sound of music from the other room ended the conversation.

"We will discuss this at home. Go now."

Olivia walked away from her mother and her friends, determined not to dance with the lecherous Lord Collingwood again. Unfortunately, she had little choice when Lord Collingwood presented himself for their second dance. The dance was a reel, and partners swapped at intervals. That meant that Lord Collingwood had no opportunity to hold her too close, and the other ladies shared the joy of having him leer at their breasts. Olivia could see similarities between being left to fend for herself against Chamberlain and now Collingwood. When he pulled her too close in the waltz and leered at her breasts, where was her mother? What had she thought when she agreed to dance and chat with whichever gentleman sought her out?

Olivia had one more name on her card, and after that dance, she wanted to go home but doubted that he sister would be agreeable. How was it possible for her mother and sister to disappear into a crowded ballroom? Was it inappropriate to go into the cardroom to look for her Father? With a sigh, Olivia realised that it would be frowned upon, and the old biddies who already thought she was fast would condemn her further. She chose a seat away from the dance floor and resigned herself to a long wait.

Seated with the wallflowers, Olivia dropped the fake smile she had pasted on her face all evening and relaxed against the back of the chair. Ladies were required to sit up straight in public, but Olivia felt sure that none of the guests bothered to look over at the wallflowers during the evening unless it was to smirk at them. Lady Agnes walked towards Olivia and sank onto a chair.

"Goodness, my feet ache. I swear I've had my toes trodden on at least a dozen times. Some gentlemen have more enthusiasm than ability. Why are you hiding over here?"

"I have no more dance partners, and I have no wish to chat to Lord Collingwood, so I should be safe if he doesn't look over here. The man makes my skin crawl. Why are debutantes not allowed to decline a dance when a gentleman asks?"

"I don't know. It's one of those stupid rules the old biddies insist we must follow. When I grow up, I want to be a bad fairy, and I will attend an event and smite the old biddies down with my magic wand."

Olivia chuckled. "Make sure you invite me when you are ready for smiting."

Lady Agnes said, "I can't understand why those old crows sit along the edge of the dance floor looking for transgressions. Does it make them happy to ruin debutants with their rulings?"

"And it doesn't matter how badly behaved the men are; the debutant shoulders the blame. Imagine spending years learning how to behave and present yourself, only to be banned by the old biddies because you are too fast. To my knowledge, no man has ever had to answer for his misbehaviour. Why do those old crows sit and watch men like Collingwood manhandle girls without calling a halt to his conduct?"

"Do you think they are jealous, and calling out girls for unseemly behaviour makes them feel powerful? They've lost their youth and beauty, so they must make themselves noteworthy in some other way."

Olivia grimaced. "Whatever the reason, I hope I don't fall victim to their machinations."

Chapter Six

After a late night at a ball, most ladies lay in bed until lunchtime, but as a country girl, Olivia knew that if you lay abed all morning, you wasted the best part of the day. Olivia dragged herself out of bed and rang for her maid. There might be callers, so she had her maid dress her hair, and the gown she chose showed Olivia's dewy skin and dark hair to perfection.

When Olivia walked into the sitting room, the maid smiled at her.

"The messengers delivered bouquets this morning. This large one is for you. How romantic."

Olivia screwed up her face, and a feeling of dread engulfed her.

"Where is the card, Maggie?"

After hunting through the enormous bunch of flowers, Maggie found the card. The bouquet was from Lord Collingwood. Olivia's stomach rolled when she saw the name.

"Ew."

"Are you not enamoured of the gentleman, Miss?"

"Maggie, he is no gentleman. He is a lecherous swine. As I told my mother yesterday, a title doesn't make a man a gentleman."

"Do you want me to dispose of the flowers?"

Olivia sighed. "No, you'd better not in case he pays his respects." Lady Clayborne and Georgia entered the room. Georgia hunted through the bouquets until she found the card she was looking for. A smile wreathed her face, and she made her way to the settee.

"Lord Brunswick has sent flowers. I hope he calls today. Are there flowers for you, Olivia?"

"Yes, that bunch there," she said as she pointed to the massive bunch. "They are from Lord Collingwood, and I hope he doesn't call today."

Lady Clayborne tutted."We had this conversation last night. You cannot ignore him because he is an Earl."

"So, you want me to marry the bounder to be polite? Understand me, mother, no inducement on earth will encourage me to become involved with him. I have no intention of spending the rest of my life with him, sweating over me and doing lewd things. And after that fiasco at home, I'm smart enough not to get caught in a room unchaperoned. If I were married to Lord Chamberlain because you deliberately allowed the man to compromise me, I would hate you for the rest of my life. If you encourage Lord Collingwood, I will hold you responsible for whatever happens."

A knock on the door announced the butler.

"Madame, you have callers. Will I say you are receiving?"

"Yes, thank you, Grayson. Please ask Mrs Hewson to bring refreshments."

The first visitor was Lord Brunswick. He bowed to the ladies and took his place next to Georgia. Lord Collingwood, who followed him into the room, performed the same ritual and sat in the armchair nearest Olivia. A polite conversation ensued until the refreshments arrived, and then everyone took a few moments to collect the cups of tea that Lady Clayborn poured.

As Lord Collingwood rambled on, Olivia half-listened to the conversation between Georgia and Lord Brunswick. His topics for discussion ranged from Georgia's newest ribbons and bonnets to her new gowns. Was the man not able to converse on any exciting topics? The time limit for polite visits rolled around, and the gentlemen rose to leave. Before he did so, Lord Brunswick said, "Georgia, is it too presumptuous of me to ask you to ride in the park tomorrow? I bought a new chaise, and I want to try it out. Your company would be welcome."

Georgia blushed and accepted the offer. Dismay filled Olivia's stomach because Lord Brunswick had invited Georgia; Lord Collingwood would do the same.

"What an excellent idea. Will you join me for a carriage ride in the park, Miss Olivia?"

Olivia stuttered for a moment and then regained her composure.

"Thank you for the invitation, Lord Collingwood, but I have a prior engagement tomorrow."

The man did not look pleased but accepted her refusal with a grim nod.

"Maybe next time?"

Olivia smiled without agreeing, and the gentleman left.

When the door closed, Lady Clayborn glared at her daughter.

"Pray, tell us, what is your prior engagement?"

"There is no engagement, but I would prefer to clean out the chamber pots than spend time alone with that man. You seem to be having trouble understanding me, Mother. I will not pander to that man, and I will not spend time with him. If you are so fond of him, you may adopt him, but don't ever expect me to marry the man. I'm at a loss to understand your fascination with a man whose only attribute is his title. Please excuse me; I need to speak to Father."

Olivia stalked along the hallway to her father's office. His door was ajar "Can I speak with you, Father?"

Lord Clayborn looked up at his daughter and smiled.

"Come in, my dear. What can I do for you?"

"I know we disagreed about you permitting Chamberlain to woo me, but I hope we've agreed about who I want to spend time with and who I don't."

"And this is someone you don't want to spend time with?"

Olivia told her father of the lecherous earl and her mother's insistence that she not insult the man.

"Mother introduced Lord Collingwood to Georgia and me at the garden party. She seems to have no ability to see the worth of a man who has a title. The man is sweaty and never looks me in the eyes; he fixes his gaze on my chest. He puts his name on my card twice every time we go to a ball, and always the one before supper, so I must spend time with him. He is disrespectful, and the way he grips me when we dance draws attention. The old biddies sit along the wall and gossip about how fast I am. Could you please talk to Mother? If the man comes to ask if he can court me, please tell him I have no interest in furthering our acquaintance.

Lord Clayborne gazed at his daughter.

"Well, that sounds like you have a problem. In one way, your mother is right; you shouldn't insult an Earl. However, if he is disrespectful and calls your reputation into question, it is best to steer clear of him. I will speak with your mother about doing a better job of supervising you. We might deflect him that way."

"And the courting thing?"

"I will tell the man that his attentions are not welcome."

"Thank you, Father."

Tonight was the first social event since Olivia had talked to her father about Lord Collingwood, so she assumed that her mother would stay close and be vigilant in her chaperoning duties. As the group entered the ballroom, Olivia gripped her mother's hand.

"Please do not disappear tonight. I need you to stand near me so the earl is on his best behaviour."

"I'm sure there will be no problems tonight. After the last event, I am certain Lord Collingwood has considered his behaviour. I will keep you company while gentlemen fill in your dance card."

"I need you to stand here if I dance with the earl. Your presence might stop him from being disrespectful."

"Goodness, dear, you complain. Let's mingle."

As the ladies walked through the crowds of people, Olivia kept an eye out for the earl. She hoped to avoid him for most of the night. She realised her wish was not to come true as three men approached their group. Lord Brunswick bowed over her mother's hand, greeted her coolly, and greeted Georgia effusively. Behind Lord Brunswick were Mr Smithton, a second son, and Lord Collingwood. Mr Smithton greeted all three ladies and placed his name on both dance cards. Lord Collingwood sidled up next to Olivia. She moved away, only to have him follow. When she gave her mother a desperate glance, her mother was chatting to Lord Brunswick, oblivious to her daughter's plight.

"Mother, I need help."

Her mother glanced at her. Olivia looked panicked, trapped against the crowd behind her and Lord Collingwood, who stood too close. Lady Claybourne looked at Lord Collingwood with a frown.

"Lord Collingwood, move away from my daughter. I cannot imagine what you're doing standing so close. It is improper, and you are upsetting my daughter. If you intend to write on her dance card, please do and then move away."

Lord Collingwood scowled at Lady Clayborne and then grabbed Olivia's card. When the man walked away, she heaved a sigh of relief.

"Thank you, Mother. The man is insufferable. I would have preferred it if you had not allowed him to place his name on my dance card."

Once her card was full, Olivia stepped onto the dance floor with her partner. Dance after dance followed, and in the brief break between sets, Lord Collingwood again approached Olivia. Her mother was nowhere in sight, and she had no choice but to converse with the man. When the MC announced the next dance, Lord Collingwood extended his arm.

"This is my dance, Miss Olivia."

The dance was bearable because it was progressive, and Lord Collingwood had no opportunity to leer or grope her.

"I will return for my next dance in a while."

Before she could check on the odious man's claim, her partner arrived and escorted her onto the dance floor.

After her second and final dance with the earl, Olivia stood with the other debutants, waiting for their partners. A hush fell over the ballroom. A tide of silence started at the front of the room and swept through like a tidal wave. The girls craned their necks to see what was happening when whispers passed from person to person.

"What on earth is happening?" Olivia asked.

Her friend, Agnes, hissed, "Turn away. It's the scandalous Duke of Nottingham. He is sinfully handsome and filthy rich, and he dallies with the widows and bored married ladies. He has a dreadful reputation. He is looking for a bride, but none of the ton mamas will sacrifice their daughters because of his reputation. If he were to talk to a woman, the ton would have the rumours circulating before supper."

"Why is he scandalous?"

Agnes rolled her eyes in an unladylike manner.

"They say that he gambles and drinks and entertains widows and actresses."

Olivia laughed. "The ton dowagers whisper that I am fast because Lord Collingwood gropes and leers at me. I wonder how much of the Duke's reputation is fiction and how much is fact?"

"Well, it's not something that has to worry us. Our chaperones will not introduce us to such a notorious man."

Olivia looked around the room. "That assumes that one can find their chaperone. Mine is very obvious by her absence."

Olivia had no partner for the dance before supper and prepared herself to eat with the other unaccompanied ladies when Lord Collingwood appeared.

"Miss Olivia, I believe this dance is mine."

Stunned, she stared at the man. "We have had two dances, and I will not dance with you a third time."

"Don't be bashful. Come on now."

When Lord Collingwood grabbed her arm, Olivia tried to pull out of his grasp.

"If we dance a third time, I will wake up in the morning to read of my betrothal. Let me go, Lord Collingwood."

"After we dance a third time, you are correct. Our betrothal will be public, and I get the most delicious debutant of the year and your healthy dowry." The man gave a nasty laugh.

In desperation, Olivia looked around for her mother. The dratted woman wasn't anywhere around. Her gaze locked on the infamous Duke, and she mouthed the words, "Help me." He nodded and ducked his head towards the man next to him. The man looked over his shoulder and said something to the Duke. Damn it, no help from that quarter.

"Let go, you oaf. I will scream if you continue to shove me. I'd rather cause a scandal than become betrothed to you."

A deep voice said, "No scandal required."

The Duke glared at Collingwood.

"Take your hand off the young lady, you cad, or I will break your arm."

When Collingwood removed his hand, the Duke held out his arm.

"Would you do me the honour, Miss Olivia?"

Olivia placed her hand on his arm, and he escorted her to the ballroom. The couple danced for a few minutes.

"Are you all right? What happened there?"

In a shaky voice, Olivia relayed the incident. She confided in the Duke about her difficulties whenever she attended a social event.

"My mother, damn her, was to keep the man away. She disappears at every event we go to, and if I didn't know better, I'd assume she was meeting a lover."

The Duke grinned for a minute. "Do ladies of the ton say 'damn'?"

A blush rushed up Olivia's face. "I beg your pardon, my lord."

"Let us further our acquaintance. I know, because I asked, that you are Miss Olivia Clayborne, the second daughter of Edward Clayborne. I am Charles Duprais, the Duke of Nottingham."

"Thank you for saving me, my lord."

"Sweetheart, I'm not so sure you should thank me. You have now gained another fault by dancing with me. If the dowagers thought you were fast before, now they will question your virtue."

"If the old biddies helped instead of starting rumours, the ballroom would be safer. Who knew that a cad could compromise a debutante in the middle of the dance floor? I no longer care what they say about me; I know I have done nothing wrong. And I'm glad you can read lips from across the room because I intended to scream. Involvement in a scandal is preferable to a lifetime of misery married to that man."

"Has he accosted you before? How did you meet such a disreputable man? Aren't chaperones supposed to protect the debutants?"

"I met him at the garden party because my mother introduced him. She thinks I want a man with a title, and his character doesn't matter. Before we arrived, she tried to have a long-time friend of my father compromise me, supposedly so that I could stay in the country because I complained about coming to town. That man is old, fat and has a nasty temper. His first wife died unexpectedly, and there was some talk that he killed her. See how discerning my mother is when choosing companions to accompany me? I clarified that I won't marry some scoundrel just because he has a title."

"So, a title doesn't matter to you?"

"No, a title doesn't make a man a gentleman. I'm tempted to ask my father to find another chaperone for me, but I would have to tell him that my mother leaves Georgia and me unattended for most of the evening. I don't want to cause discord between my parents, but my mother jeopardises my reputation by allowing a cad like Collingwood to dance with me."

"Hm, I see your problem."

"I don't understand why she finds unsuitable men to be my suitors, but she leaves Georgia to her own devices. It hardly seems fair that I must deflect unsuitable men while Georgia is blithely unaware."

"Is that a hint? Should I take my leave?"

Chapter Seven

The music stopped, and Olivia chewed her bottom lip as she looked at Charles. She glanced over her shoulder; Lord Collingwood stood glaring at the couple.

"That is not your cue to leave; could you damage my reputation some more by escorting me to supper? I fear Lord Collinwood will try something else to force me to marry him once you are not next to me."

Charles looked at his unexpected dance partner. He held out his arm and patted her hand when she placed it in his.

"My dear, it will be my pleasure to ruin your reputation by escorting you to supper."

The supper room was overflowing; all the dancers were relaxing and refreshing. Charles steered her towards a small table at the back of the room.'

"Forgive me. The table is a poor choice, but none of these folks wants to eat with me. I could force the issue, but I won't embarrass you anymore."

While Charles collected food and drinks, Olivia looked around her. Friends and acquaintances took furtive glances at her and whispered behind their fans. She scanned the crowd, looking for her mother and sister. Her eyes focused on a couple sitting at the back of the room on the opposite side. Her mother conversed deeply with a good-looking older man, and when she laid her hand on his, Olivia's jest about a secret lover looked true.

Charles's arrival with the food distracted her. For the next thirty minutes, they shared confidences and hopes. Olivia never found the men of the ton easy to talk with. They discussed new ribbons and embroidery, as well as their companions' new dresses. Did they assume women could not converse about more meaningful topics?

"The talk of the ton when you walked in was that you need a bride. What has made you ready to settle, if I may be so bold? Or do you intend to put your wife at one of your country estates and continue with your carousing?"

"You realise that I avoided answering every time someone asked that question? I'm not sure why I want to tell you and why I know you won't share what I say with the gossip mongers of the ton."

He raised his eyebrows at Olivia, and she grinned.

"I always wonder how men do that with their eyebrows." Her face took on a grave expression. "What you tell me will go no further. I am the topic of gossip now, and what the dowagers say is not true. So, what you say will go no further."

Charles nodded. "As I grew up, my father expected me to learn how to run the estate. It was my destiny, but even though he was firm but fair, I chaffed at the restrictions of all that responsibility. When I reached my majority, I thought I knew everything I needed to, and I went wild. I had too much alcohol, too much gambling and mixed with the wrong women."

He glanced at Olivia.

"I beg your pardon. My conversation is not suitable for a lady."

"Piffle, my lord. Finish the story."

An amused expression crossed the Duke's face, and then he continued.

"After a lengthy absence, I received a letter from my father's steward. He apologised for interfering but thought he should tell me that my father was seriously ill. I high-tailed it back home to find my father dying. Guilt ate at me. I could have removed the burden from my father's shoulders while he was sick, but I lived a dissolute life in the city. His one wish was to see me married, so I cleaned up my act after his death and hit the social scene. The ridiculous thing is that the debutants' mamas run away from me, but I've not found a debutant I want to marry, let alone live alongside for the rest of my life."

"I am sorry for your difficulties. I wish you well in your search.".

"Enough of me. Tell me about you."

For the next fifteen minutes, they discussed books and favourite authors. Olivia admitted that her favourite author was E.V. Hayes.

"Imagine having to take a pen name and pretend to be male to get your books published. She has another one out, but I can't locate it in any bookshop. I'm unsure if it is popular or if the revelation that she is a woman has stopped the booksellers from stocking her book."

Olivia looked up. The room was emptying fast as people moved to the dance floor. She spied her mother as the woman crossed the room.

"Mother. Lady Clayborne!"

Lady Clayborne stopped, and her gaze zeroed in on Charles. He stood and introduced himself,

"Lady Clayborne, we have a problem we need to discuss, so somewhere more private might be best."

Olivia's mother's expression hardened. "If you are with my daughter, I can imagine the problem. You escorting her to tea will ruin her reputation more than anyone else could."

"Mother, stop! Lord Duprais came to my rescue while you kept company with a man. You cannot discuss ruined reputations when you do not know what has occurred. You can meet as many lovers as you see fit, but your primary role is as a chaperone. I doubt you can chaperone anyone from a bedroom. Please listen to what we say."

Charles watched in fascination as Olivia took her mother to task. The woman's face was an entertaining kaleidoscope of embarrassment, anger and guilt.

"Please, can we find a quiet place to talk?"

Lady Clayborne inclined her head in a gesture of consent. It took very few minutes to bring her up to speed. Charles frowned at the woman who was supposed to protect her daughter from cads and fortune hunters. From the expression on the woman's face, Olivia's guess that her mother was meeting a man was accurate. While her mother dallied with a man, Olivia struggled to maintain her reputation, and the woman who was supposed to supervise was unaware of the danger her daughter faced. Charles shook his head in disgust.

"I am to attend another event, so I need to leave shortly. For Olivia's safety, you need to go now. I can call your carriage if you collect your other daughter."

Lady Clayborne nodded and then disappeared amongst the crowd. A few minutes later, she returned with her daughter and Lord Brunswick. Brunswick strode in front of Georgia and pushed into Charles's face as they returned.

"What is happening, Duprais? Scaring a woman with ridiculous tales is a low act."

Before Charles could speak, Olivia interrupted.

"Lord Brunswick, this problem is a family matter, and as you're not family, it does not warrant your opinion."

Olivia turned to her sister and said, "Georgia, I must leave now. Please don't make this any more difficult. Mother, please tell Georgia that we need to leave. I can explain everything in the carriage."

"Dear Lord, Collingwood will do the right thing now that the Duke has spoken to him. I can't see any need to leave."

Charles scowled at the woman. "Madam, I hope your lover is worth ruining your daughter's reputation for. Will you be happy when you wake up tomorrow to discover that Olivia has become betrothed to that fortune hunter, Collingwood?" Charles ignored the gasp that followed his tirade. Was the woman neglectful or simple?

Charles shook his head."Olivia, it is clear that your mother does not care for your reputation: asking your father to provide another chaperone would be wise. Did a maid come with you tonight?"

"Yes."

"Good, find her, and I will call my carriage. I will escort you home."

Lady Claybourne wrung her hands.

"Accompanying that cad will ruin your reputation faster than Lord Collinwood's unwanted attentions. Please, Olivia, stay, and I will watch over you."

Olivia shook her head. "You have had every opportunity to do right by me, but failed. As soon as Lord Duprais leaves, you will abandon me again, I have no doubt. No, I want to go now, and if you don't call our coach, I will accept his Grace's offer."

Brunswick interjected.

"If that doesn't ruin her reputation, nothing will."

Charles snarled, "If you're so worried about her reputation, send the group on their way now. No? I didn't think so. The maid will act as a chaperone, and there will be no besmirching of reputations. Good evening to you all."

The carriage pulled to a stop outside the ballroom, and Lord Duprais helped the ladies into his vehicle. The carriage's occupants were silent as they drove through the deserted streets. Olivia was uncertain; she should make an effort to start a conversation. The duke seemed happy to remain silent, so Olivia took his lead. Charles stepped from the conveyance when the carriage stopped outside the Clayborne residence. After assisting Maggie to disembark, he held his hand out for Olivia. As she stood before him, trying to find the words, he tipped her chin up and kissed her cheek chastely. Embarrassment made her speechless. What did you say to a stranger who had rescued you twice?

"You livened up my night, Miss Olivia. I am glad we met."

"I am glad we met, too, your grace."

"Go inside, and if your father is more reasonable than your mother, talk to him."

Olivia nodded.

Grayson opened the door for Olivia and Maggie.

"You have had an early night, Miss."

"Yes. There were people there I disliked. Is my father still awake?"

"Yes, Miss. He is in the sitting room."

When Olivia entered the room, her father sat in a chair before the fire. The book on his lap lay unopened, and a glass of whisky was in his hand. He looked up in surprise.

"You are home early. Is your mother with you?"

"No, mother is not with me. She and Georgia stayed, but I felt it best if I left."

"Do I need to ask Grayson to direct the coach to return to collect your mother and your sister?"

"No. Maggie and I came home with the Duke of Nottingham. May I take a seat?"

Lord Clayborne nodded his head, and Olivia sank into a chair.

"I sense that all is not well. I want to ask questions, but it will be best if you tell me what has happened."

Olivia poured out the details of the night. She did her best to protect her mother's privacy, but advised her father that her mother had not performed her chaperone duty well. Without the Duke's help, she would have caused a scandal; there was no way she intended to wed that man.

"I will need to speak with the man. His behaviour is outrageous. How did you meet this Duke?"

"He saved me from Collingwood, and I asked him to take me to supper because I wasn't sure that the earl wouldn't pull another nasty trick."

"Do I know this Duke of Nottingham? Wasn't there talk of the heir being a dissolute waster?"

Olivia remained silent for a few moments. Charles had told her why things had changed for him, but in confidence. However, if she wanted her father to see that Charles had changed, she needed to share the bare bones of the conversation with him. How much of what Charles told her should she share with her father?

"The heir is Charles Duprais. He admits to being wild in his youth but changed his ways because his father was ill."

Lord Clayborne frowned. "I'm not sure you should mix with wastrels like him."

"Father, the Duke has amended his ways. And anyhow, Collingwood is supposed to be a gentleman, and tonight, he tried to trap me into marriage. I prefer to take my chances with the Duke, a man who knows how to behave, not with the earl. Mother seems to think that if the man has a title, he is a suitable prospective husband, and I can't seem to impress upon her that I don't care about the title. I want a man who will treat me well, someone I like and may grow to love. Can I ask you something unrelated?"

Lord Clayborne laughed. "And if I say no, will it stop you?"

"No."

"Ask away, daughter."

"I'm not the one Lord Brunswick is courting, but something about him puts me on edge. The man gives Georgia ridiculous compliments that sound rehearsed. He never discusses anything besides her new ribbons, dresses, or hat trim. He is treating her as a piece of property. And he treats me with disdain. I don't know what I've done to upset him unless he can tell I don't trust him."

"When he asked to court Georgia, I asked around the ton to get a sense of the man. Not many people knew him, but they could tell me he had two country properties and a stipend of ten thousand a year."

"I guess I should try getting over my objections to him. If he is to be my brother-in-law, I shouldn't dislike him. I think Georgia could do better."

"Maybe, but it's not your decision to make."

"I realise that, but I don't want Georgia to get her hopes up only to discover the man is not honourable. Can you conduct further investigation to ensure he is decent? Doesn't it cause concern that he was unknown before this season? How does an earl manage to remain anonymous?"

"I think I did my duty by Georgia and don't feel the need to waste extra resources to examine his circumstances further."

Chapter Eight

When Olivia entered the drawing room the following day, she discovered her mother and sister deep in conversation. She was reluctant to interrupt them, but her sister, seeing her, broke away from chatting with their mother.

"Good morning, Mother, Georgia. You are up early."

Lady Claybourne stared sternly at Olivia. "We need to discuss what happened last night."

"Mother, you didn't believe me last night; why will that change if we discuss it now? I told you everything that happened, and so did Lord Duprais, and you disregarded us both."

Dear, I was lax with my duties as a chaperone. I'm sorry for that oversight. Even though Lord Duprais was helpful last night, his help will give the dowagers and spinsters fodder for gossip. You need to be circumspect if you meet him in the future."

"Mother, the dowagers and the spinsters are gossiping now. They think I'm fast because I don't stop Lord Collingwood from holding me inappropriately close. He persists, even though I ask him to let me go."

Georgia screwed up her face. "Why don't you just shove him away?"

"Because he is too strong."

Lady Clayborne looked doubtful. "Surely not."

Olivia looked at her suspicious Mother and sister. She rose from her seat and walked to the door. Grayson stood outside, directing staff as they scurried around their duties.

"Grayson, I need you. Can you spare me a moment?"

"Certainly, Miss."

When Grayson and Olivia entered the room, Georgia looked startled.

"Bear with me, please, everyone. Grayson, I was hoping you could help me with a demonstration. Georgia, come over here."

Georgia hesitantly joined the butler and her sister in the middle of the room.

"Please take up a waltz position."

Grayson looked nervous, and Georgia was stunned.

"Please do as asked. I want to make a point."

Grayson and Georgia moved into position for a waltz.

"What next, Miss?"

"Sorry, Grayson. I apologise for asking you to do this, but for the demonstration, it is necessary. Pull Georgia in very close, and don't allow her to struggle free."

"Olivia, that is enough."

"No, Mother, we will complete the experiment because you don't believe me. Please, Grayson, go ahead."

Grayson's face turned a bright shade of red, but he pulled Georgia in close.

"Now, Georgia, try to break free of Grayson's hold. Please, Grayson, hold her tightly."

Olivia watched as Georgia struggled. "Do you surrender?"

"Yes, yes. Please let me go, Grayson. Olivia, you have made your point."

"Thank you, Grayson. I'm sorry to put you through that."

"Will that be all, Miss Olivia?"

Olivia laughed. "Can you tell Mrs Heatherington that we will need refreshments if we have visitors?"

Olivia faced her mother and sister. "Georgia, why didn't you shove Grayson away? After all, you suggested I should do with Lord Collingwood."

"That's enough, Olivia. You made your point."

"Well, now that I've made my point, don't you think closer surveillance by you would help solve the problem?"

Maggie knocked and entered the room. She gave a curtsy and smiled.

"A messenger delivered a lovely bunch of flowers for you, Miss."

Olivia rose from her seat and read the attached card. Her face screwed up in distaste.

"Maggie, please remove the flowers. Put them somewhere I can't see them. Give them to the cook, keep them for yourself, or discard them as you see fit. I don't care. Please give that card to Grayson. If Lord Collingwood calls, ask Grayson to direct him to Father. He is not to enter the sitting room."

Maggie hurried out of the room to do her mistress's bidding. When they heard a visitor arrive, all three women held their breath. Grayson opened the door and announced Lord Brunswick. Georgia smiled at him as he paid his respects to the three ladies. Lady Clayborne rang for the parlourmaid and asked for refreshments. Lord Brunswick sprouted platitudes and encouraged Georgia to discuss fripperies and bonnets. Olivia gritted her teeth. How could her sister bear such mundane conversations with the man she suspected could be her husband?

The refreshments arrived, and Lady Clayborne poured them for everyone. The conversation had just resumed when Grayson entered the room.

"Miss, a gentleman has delivered this parcel. He said you would understand who it was from."

Olivia took the small package. The brown paper covering the parcel gave her no clues about its origins. Pulling off the string that held the bag together, Olivia grinned. The book she had discussed with Lord Duprais last night was in her hand. On the flyleaf was a simple inscription. It read: Enjoy CD.

"Do you know the sender's origin?" her mother queried.

"Yes, I do."

She noticed Grayson hovering near the door.

"Is there a reply, Miss Olivia?"

"Did the messenger wait?"

"Yes, Miss."

Olivia followed Grayson out to the entry hallway. Charles stood there, clarifying that he was the messenger. Olivia laughed.

"You make a grand messenger, my lord. Thank you for the book. I'm not game to ask where you found it."

"Will you come with me tomorrow for a ride in my phaeton?"

"Yes, I would enjoy that."

Charles tipped his hat. "I'll see you tomorrow at ten." And with that, he departed.

Olivia delayed returning to the sitting room by taking the book to her bedroom. She could have asked a servant to do the job for her, but she wanted a few moments alone to bask in anticipation of tomorrow's excursion. Olivia placed the much sought-after book on her dressing table and grinned. Not only did she have the book she wanted, but she also had an invitation to accompany Charles the next day. With a sigh, she set down her book and her excitement and walked to the sitting room.

The other occupants looked up at her when she returned to the sitting room. Her mother broke the silence.

"Dear, who was the book from, and why did the messenger wait?"

"The book was from Lord Duprais, and the messenger waited because his grace delivered the book himself."

Lord Brunswick sneered. "What kind of gift is a book? Ladies should only concern themselves with womanly pursuits. The man does not understand the way gentlewomen live."

"Lord Brunswick, the gift was thoughtful. I have tried to buy the book myself with no luck. We discussed books at supper last night, and Lord Duprais found a copy this morning. The gift was most welcome."

Lady Clayborne looked aghast. "How could you discuss books? Everyone will think you are a bluestocking. What hope will you have of finding a husband?"

"Should Lord Duprais and I have been like Lord Brunswick, discussing new gowns or the ribbons I have bought? You, sir, insult Georgia by always discussing inconsequential topics. How is my sister supposed to get to know you if all you prattle on about are buttons and bows? Or is that the idea? What she doesn't know won't hurt her?"

After a glare at Olivia, Lord Brunswick rose and said, "It appears my company is not welcome." Lord Brunswick bowed to Georgina and Lady Clayborne, and, disregarding Olivia, he stalked from the room.

"Why do you argue with him, Olivia? If all goes well, he might become your brother-in-law, and I'm certain it upsets Georgia that you dislike her suitor."

"Mother, he has treated me with disdain from the first time we met, and his attitude has not improved with longer acquaintance."

Turning her attention to Georgia, Olivia said, " I can't believe you want to discuss ribbons and bonnets for the rest of your life, Georgia. The man is as dull as brown paper, and his compliments sound false and practised. He is the first man you've met; wouldn't it be better to get to know other men as well?"

"I dance with others, but Lord Brunswick makes me feel special. Please don't argue with him, Olivia. It makes me uncomfortable."

Olivia sighed and nodded her head. There was nothing to be gained by upsetting her sister, and from now on, she intended to steer clear of Brunswick.

Chapter Nine

Olivia glanced once more in the mirror, checking on her appearance.

"You look lovely, Miss," Maggie said.

"Oh, Maggie, I am so excited. I have had to dance with fortune hunters and ancient men and smile at them, hanging on their every word. Lord Duprais interests me. It's not just his looks; it has nothing to do with his title. He is engaging and kind. If he hadn't intervened, I would now be betrothed to that frog or shunned because of the scandal I caused."

"So, you had better go downstairs now, or he will arrive and think you are not going."

As Olivia descended, a knock came at the door. When Grayson answered it, her pulse spiked. She was giddy with excitement. With a smile at Grayson, she accepted the extended arm and accompanied Lord Duprais to the phaeton. Once they settled into the conveyance, Lord Duprais took the reins from a stable lad.

"If you agree, I thought we might choose the least travelled path in the park."

Olivia's heart fell. He didn't want anyone to see them together. Tears welled in her eyes, and she lowered her head.

"Yes," was all she said.

He set the horses into a steady trot, only slowing when they came to the turnoff. The horses plodded along, and the silence between Olivia and the Duke became strained. When the conveyance stopped, Lord Duprais turned to her.

"Are you going to tell me what is wrong? The ride excited you when you hopped in, but now you are unhappy."

"My lord, why did you ask me to join you if you want to hide that we are together? Why ask me if it embarrasses you for people to see us together?"

"What the devil are you talking about? I am not embarrassed."

"Then why choose a track few people frequent?"

"You silly goose. I chose this track so I could be alone with you. Turn around and look at me."

Olivia turned in her seat. Charles looked grave, his brown eyes open and honest.

"I want to find a wife. Of all the young ladies I might marry, you are the only one to pique my interest. I want to get to know you, but I don't want the ton to speculate on our association. I am hiding you, but my reasons are honourable."

He ran his finger along her cheek, the caress causing Olivia to inhale. The sensation his fingers caused made her tremble.

"You feel it too, don't you?"

Olivia couldn't find words; her voice had deserted her. But she nodded.

"Tell me of this obsession Collingwood has with you."

"The first social event we attended, he was there. My mother, curse her, introduced us. He puts his name on my card for two dances at every event we attend. If he arrives early in the evening and my card is empty, he puts his name on my card for two waltzes. One of those is always before supper. The other night, I retreated to the ladies' room for the whole of supper, so I didn't have to sit at a table with him leering at my bosom."

Olivia blushed. "Oh dear, did I just say that in front of a gentleman?"

Charles grinned. "I can understand his wish to gaze at your breasts, but I know how crass that is of him and how angry it makes you. And your mother is no help because she seems to have a rendezvous with a gentleman somewhere private."

"The man chooses a waltz and then holds me so close that it's indecent. Instead of anyone assisting me, they all condemn me for being fast. I proved to my mother how impossible it is to get out of his grasp, but I am doomed unless I put on a display for the whole ton."

Charles turned and jumped from the carriage. When he walked around to extend his hand to Olivia, she was unsure what he had planned.

"I want to show you how to escape from the man's grasp, but I will have to grip you. Are you willing for me to show you?"

Olivia nodded. Charles pulled her towards himself and mimicked the position of a waltz. "Ready?"

"Yes."

Olivia stiffened as Lord Duprais pulled her against him. But the disgust she experienced with Lord Collingwood didn't happen with Charles. With her body pressed against his chest, Olivia yearned to stay in that position for eternity. Charles let out a growl.

"Damn, I didn't think this out very well."

He moved her back, and Olivia wanted to protest.

In a gruff voice. Lord Duprais said, "Tell me which parts of your body you can move when Collingwood holds you too tight."

"Ah, my head and my legs?"

"Right. Lift your leg so that your bent knee is close to my body. If you push your knee forward, where would it hit me?"

A blush raced across Olivia's face. "Um, in your man parts?"

"Yes, and if you do that fast, he will drop to the floor crying. You need to turn and walk away. Everyone will be too busy focusing on him rolling around on the ground to pay attention to you."

"My skirts will hide my legs, so nobody will know what happened. That's brilliant."

Charles still clasped Olivia in his arms.

"Ah, my lord, you ought to let me go. What if somebody comes along this track?"

The Duke laughed. "Well, then, I would have my bride chosen for me. There is one other move, but it will be obvious to those around you. As a last resort, a headbutt may be an effective option. You slam your head against his face, either his nose or forehead."

"But the man looks at my, ah, breasts. I don't see his face."

The sound of a horse's hooves hurried Charles into helping Olivia into the carriage. By the time the riders came into sight, the duke had sat in the moving carriage. He pulled aside to allow the horses to pass, then turned the phaeton toward home. Unlike the journey out, there was no lack of conversation on the return trip. When Charles helped Olivia alight from the phaeton, she was smitten. After escorting her to the door, the Duke asked her to join him on a walk the following day. Unless he intended to walk her among the trees, it appeared that Charles had decided to let everyone know they were spending time together. The thought made Olivia giddy with excitement.

Over the next week, Charles and Olivia spent part of every day together. They walked in the park late in the afternoon to stop the gossipers speculating; they rode early in the morning and had refreshments in the garden. One afternoon, as they strolled through the gardens, Maggie followed behind at a scant distance to chaperone the couple. Olivia asked, "My Lord, what are we doing?"

"What do you mean? We are walking in the garden."

"My mother asked if we were courting, and I know you haven't seen my father, so what are we doing?"

"My apologies, my dear. Once we agree to court, the outcome is inevitable, so I wanted to take the opportunity to get to know you. Our time together has been enjoyable; we will complement each other well. I will speak to your father."

Charles pulled her along, and she followed, unsure of his intentions. Charles pulled her into his arms when the shrubbery hid them from Maggie.

"I intend to kiss you. If you don't want that, speak now."

Olivia smiled and lifted on her tiptoes; her face turned towards his. Charles lowered his head, his lips brushing across her lips fleetingly.

Olivia sounded frustrated, and Charles responded by crushing his mouth against hers. Nothing was polite about the kiss; it was all heat and hunger. Olivia held onto Charles's lapels, needing something to help her stand. Maggie's voice broke the spell, and Charles straightened his coat and offered her his arm.

Much to her dismay, when Olivia entered the house, her father was out on business, so the Duke's request to court her had to wait another day. Her mother and Georgia were in the small parlour, entertaining, so she went to join them. Grayson opened the door for her, and she realised the visitor was Lord Brunswick. The man droned on about his estates and his horses. It was too late to retreat, so Olivia moved into the room.

"Olivia, did you have a pleasant walk?"

Her beaming smile was an answer, but she said,

"Yes, thank you, mother."

Lord Brunswick had ceased his self-involved conversation to glare at her.

"You aren't still walking out with that degenerate, are you? I can't understand why your parents allow you to ruin your reputation by associating with a wastrel. If you ruin your reputation, you damage Georgia's. I won't have it. I must speak to your father to rectify things."

Olivia glared at Lord Brunswick.

"How dare you? You are not correct about the man that Lord Duprais is, but you have no right to tell me what to do. You may become my brother-in-law, but I will never like you. Pardon, Mother, I will take my leave."

Olivia stormed from the sitting room and stomped her way to her bedroom. How could the man turn her magic afternoon to dust in such a brief time? Olivia wanted to bask in the enjoyment of her afternoon, but the spectre of Lord Brunswick loomed. She didn't understand why the man disliked her. His attitude contributed to their arguments; he preferred his woman to be subservient and meek. Olivia was neither. Could he cause trouble between her and Charles? She hoped her father was immune to threats by Lord Brunswick. If he were to conclude his courtship with Georgia, it might be best.

As she descended the stairs the following day, doors opened and closed around her. The loud reverberation of a slammed door caused her to jump. Grayson looked flustered, something she had never seen. With a thoughtful expression, she headed for the breakfast room. When her mother and Georgia looked up, guilt and remorse showed on their faces.

"What on earth is going on, and why do you two look so strange?"

Georgia shook her head.

"I'm sorry, Olivia, but you shouldn't argue with him."

"Is that comment supposed to make sense? Who shouldn't I argue with, and why are you sorry?"

Grayson stepped into the breakfast room.

"Miss, Lord Clayborne wishes to speak to you. He is in his study."

Olivia cast a curious eye at her sister and mother and followed Grayson to the study. Her father sat in the bulky chair behind his desk, wearing an expression of anger.

"Goodness, everyone is out of sorts this morning."

Olivia watched as her father straightened papers and fiddled with his pens. When he turned his attention to her, he said,

"Lord Duprais called this morning to ask my permission to court you."

Olivia beamed. "That should make mother happy. He is the only man who has interested me since the season started, and he will make an excellent partner and husband."

"I told him no."

Olivia stood in stunned silence. Did her father say that he refused Charles's suit? Tears welled in her eyes. "What? How could you do that? Did you think I didn't want him to court me? Send a message; tell him we got our wires crossed."

"I'm sorry, I can't do that. Lord Brunswick informed me that he would cease to court Georgia if you continued to keep company with the

Duke. He insists that your association with the Duke will ruin your reputation and, consequently, Georgia's."

"He's a hateful, boring man. Call his bluff. Georgia could do better than him. What happens if he marries Georgia? Will you allow him to pick my suitors?"

"I'm sorry. Georgia has set her heart on the man."

"What of me? I have set my heart on Lord Duprais. Is her future more important than mine?"

"You will have other opportunities later or even next season."

"I don't want other opportunities. I want Charles."

Olivia raced from the room. As she passed the breakfast room, she glared at her sister.

"Your beau is a hateful, dull, busybody. How can you want to spend the rest of your life with a man who thinks you are too stupid to discuss anything other than your latest gown or the ribbons you bought? Because of him, I had to give up the one man who interested me. The person I am seeing should not make him reconsider his choice if he is genuinely enamoured of you. His ultimatum means that while you are happy, I am losing the one man in this damn town that interests me. If you marry that man, don't count me in your wedding party and don't expect me to visit you at your estate. I never thought a man would come between us, but I was wrong."

As Olivia stormed from the room, Georgia sighed.

"I know this isn't fair, but Lord Brunswick made his concerns known to me a while ago. I don't see that it matters because even if being courted by the Duke ruins Olivia, it doesn't stand to reason that the disgrace will flow to me. Is Olivia right? Should Lord Brunswick not be reluctant to marry me regardless of who is courting my sister?"

Lady Claybourne nodded. "Yes, I believe she is right, but your beau seems less tolerant than others. I agree about the ruination. Your father believes Lord Brunswick, so there is little we can do about it. What's done is done, and we must live with the consequences."

Georgia frowned. "Yes, but that consequence means Olivia is heartbroken. I will talk to Lord Brunswick and see if he will relent, but I don't hold much hope."

Chapter Ten

Hours of crying left Olivia's face puffy and red. Her swollen eyes ached, and her heart hurt. At the start of the season, she resigned herself to marrying a man for his title and money. She hoped that the man her parents chose was at least likable. Her parents assured her that if she liked her intended, that was the best outcome she ought to expect. Never had she thought to find a handsome, charming man who enthralled her and who was interested in her.

Olivia missed lunch, unable to face food or her sister. When Maggie entered her room, carrying the blue dress she would wear tonight, Olivia waved her away.

"I don't need that, Maggie, because I don't intend to go tonight."

"I can help with the damage from the crying. You will look lovely tonight."

"And if mother is her usual appalling chaperone, I will come home betrothed to that slimy earl. No, thank you. I am not attending."

Upon Maggie's departure, Lady Clayborne barrelled into the room.

"Goodness, child. I don't need the hysterics. Let Maggie help you dress and fix your face. I will not be late because of your tantrum."

"Don't let me hold up your affair. Is the man you are meeting the man you had the intimate conversation with at supper the night of the Oxenham's ball? Father says I have to find a husband next season, so that's what I'll do. I'm not going. Without Lord Duprais's protection, I will be betrothed to Lord Collingwood tomorrow morning. I would sooner shoot myself than live a life of misery with that bounder. Go to the ball, Mother. Enjoy your rendezvous, and leave me alone."

"This is absurd. I will speak to your father, who will insist you go."

"Speak to Father, but understand that I will tell him about the lover you meet instead of chaperoning Georgia and me."

Lady Clayborne's face flushed an ugly red, and she stalked out of the room.

"Close the door on your way out. I don't wish to talk with anyone."

For the following week, Olivia spent hours in the garden, and as night fell, she retreated to her room. If her family could treat her in such an unfeeling way, she wanted nothing to do with them. She took her meals on a tray in her room and never ventured too far from her bedroom at night. Her time spent alone gave her no peace. She longed to see Charles and wondered if he was searching for another debutant. The thought that he might seek another woman scorched her heart. He had confided that he wished to marry to honour his father's last request, so he would not dally waiting for Lord Clayborne to change his mind. After giving Lord Brunswick a spray, Olivia did not enter the sitting room when Georgia and her mother entertained guests. There was no one she wanted to see, and she had no desire to engage in polite chitchat with acquaintances.

Seated in the garden, she spied a man walking toward her. When he got closer, Olivia realised it was Lord Brunswick. She sneered at the man.

"Go away and leave me in peace. You got what you wanted, so leave."

"I wanted you to know that the gentleman you were walking out with has spent the last two weeks at a brothel, drinking and gambling. You should thank me for my intervention." Lord Brunswick smirked.

"I will never thank you. You are as slimy as Lord Collingwood. God help my sister if she were to marry you. Her misery will last a lifetime."

The news that Charles had returned to his wastrel ways was not news to Olivia. She expected his hard work to turn his reputation around, but it had not worked; he would see no purpose in continuing his reform. As the days dragged on, Brunswick smirked at her when he saw her. She wondered if the man had an alternative agenda, one that extended beyond disrupting her life. Snippets of conversation floated to her occasionally, and Olivia grew concerned that Brunswick was attempting to coerce Georgia into eloping. Olivia knew that if she aired her concerns with her father, he would assume it was sour grapes on her part. How could she stop this disaster before it became the year's greatest scandal? Not to mention the ruination of Georgia's future and happiness?

She trusted one person with this information, but her father had banned her from contacting Charles. Who in the household could she trust to keep her secret if she tried to visit him? She would need an unmarked carriage and a driver who would respect her privacy and refrain from gossiping. Over the next few days, Olivia mulled over whom to trust to help her contact Charles. She knew she needed to take a risk, so she tracked Grayson down in the kitchen.

"Grayson, can I speak to you in private?"

Grayson's usually expressionless face showed momentary surprise before returning to his poker face.

"Certainly, Miss Olivia."

Olivia explained to Grayson her concern about Lord Brunswick and her need to have the man investigated, despite her father's opinion that he had done enough. She asked him to help secure an unmarked carriage and a trustworthy driver so that she could visit Charles and ask him to inquire about Brunswick.

"I know I am asking a lot, but I'm not sure who in the staff I can trust. If you refuse my request, you will not share the information with anyone else. Can you help me?"

Grayson nodded. "There's something about that cove that doesn't sit right. Please leave it to me. I'll arrange a carriage and driver for tomorrow night. You might want to wear a cloak with a hood to disguise yourself, and we'll leave your departure until everyone is in bed."

"Thank you. I'll be as speedy as I can. I will feel better when I share this problem with someone else."

Grayson tapped on Olivia's door after the house fell silent. Olivia donned her cloak and covered her head with the hood before walking along the driveway a short distance. Grayson, concerned about the noise of the wheels or the jingle of the harness that might give the game away, had told the driver to wait for Olivia away from the house. The carriage rolled silently along the driveway, and when they reached the street, the driver moved the team along. The roads were empty and silent at this time of night, and for that, Olivia was grateful. She needed to see Charles, and for the mission to succeed, the fewer people who knew, the better.

The small carriage pulled to a stop in front of the house. A shrouded, hooded figure stepped from the coach. The conveyance moved further along the street after a whispered conversation between the driver and occupant. When the butler answered the door, Olivia shocked him by asking to speak to the Duke.

"Madam, his grace is in bed. If you come back tomorrow, he might be receiving."

"If I could return tomorrow with my maid to escort me, I would. Please, I must speak urgently with Lord Duprais."

The butler hesitated. When she spoke, the quality of her voice was easy to recognise. Was this woman, not a light skirt, intent on pleasuring the master, but a lady of quality? Hunter was rarely flummoxed, but the dilemma he faced was one he had never experienced. Did he assume this lady was telling the truth, and that the reason for visiting the Duke was crucial? Against his better judgment, Hunter stepped aside to let the woman enter.

Who shall I say is calling?"

Olivia laughed. "My apologies, but I needn't disguise myself if I give you my name."

"Excellent, Madam. Allow me to inform his grace that you are here."

Olivia paced, her nerves causing her anxiety. What if Charles refused to see her? She might have to reveal her name and risk ruining her reputation. Olivia watched as the butler walked away, her heart racing at the daring meeting she had organised. When the butler reached Charles's bedroom, it was clear that his master had over-imbibed. Since the father of the woman, his grace had desired to court, had turned him down, the number of sober nights was minimal.

"My Lord, a woman in the foyer says she must speak to you."

Charles groaned. A night of heavy drinking left him hungover and angry. His common sense told him that his drunken behaviour was not the way to get Olivia back, but he was at a loss to develop a good plan.

"Tell her to come back tomorrow."

"I'm sorry, my lord. I told her to come back tomorrow, but she said that if she could return with her maid tomorrow, she would, but that is not a choice."

"Tell her I will allow her entrance if she gives her name."

"My lord, I asked for her name, and she laughed. She said if she gave her name, she needn't bother disguising herself."

Charles levered himself out of bed with a sigh. "Send her up here, and she can say her piece, then leave. I have no patience for light skirts trying to trick their way into my home."

"Ah, my lord, this woman is a lady. Might I suggest you meet her somewhere other than in your bedroom?"

Charles cocked his head. "A lady, you say?"

"Yes, my lord."

"Very well, show her into the parlour. I will be there in a minute."

When the parlour door opened, Olivia turned. Charles wore an unbuttoned linen shirt and his breeches, and the sight was breathtaking and improper.

"Madam, Hunter tells me you wish to discuss an urgent issue with me. Please state your business and leave."

Olivia removed her hood. The heavy silence caused her to wonder if this had been an outstanding idea.

"Olivia. Dear God. Are you mad? Is it you?"

"I am sane, but I need your help."

"Do you want refreshments?"

"No, thank you. My carriage is outside waiting, and I don't want to call attention to myself."

"Tell me the door has no crest."

Olivia laughed. "Maybe you are the mad person! I didn't bring the family carriage. Anyhow, enough of that. I need your help. Besides being a nasty, vindictive ass, something is not right with Lord Brunswick. When my Father asked about his contacts, nobody knew the man, but they said he had country estates and a stipend of ten thousand pounds a year. But at the moment, he is pressuring Georgia into eloping, and I suspect it might be because he fears disclosure of some wrongdoing relating to his activities."

"I never liked the bounder. Can't you warn your father of the proposed elopement?"

"My father would attribute it to sour grapes on my part. Since he refused your request to court me, I refuse to attend any social events. He told me I could find a beau next season, so I use that excuse when he complains of my lack of social engagements."

"Why are you not attending events?"

Olivia pulled a face. "For the same reason, you are over-imbibing."

Charles stood and stalked to where she stood. She tilted his head towards him when his hand tangled in her hair. Charles's lips crashed on hers, his hand now wrapped around her waist. Her exploring hand ran over the firm expanse of his chest, and she snuggled closer. A knock on the door broke the spell.

"My lord, the lady needs to leave. Her carriage will cause people to ask questions if she stays much longer."

"Give me a minute, and then she will be ready to leave."

When Hunter left, Charles pulled Olivia in for a hug.

"Tell me you won't use your knee on me."

Her smile warmed his heart. "No, never."

"You had best go, and I will do all I can to investigate Brunswick. What should I do then?"

"Visit my father, tell him all you know, and demand to court me. If that fails, will you elope with me?"

His grin caused tingling to ripple across her skin.

"Madam, I am always at your disposal."

He kissed her and opened the door.

Hunter bowed at the now-cloaked and hooded figure. He glanced at Charles and said, "Your Grace, I should help the lady to her carriage. I don't believe anybody is awake at this hour, but if someone should look this way, your white shirt will stand out."

Charles nodded his consent, and Hunter whistled. The sound of the horses' hooves echoed in the night's silence. With Hunter's help, Olivia entered the coach, and a moment later, they were on their way.

As Olivia travelled back through the streets she had so recently traversed, she hoped her request would garner results. She smiled and touched her lips. Charles' kisses were delicious, and she looked forward to more when her suitor revealed what he had discovered about Brunswick.

Chapter Eleven

Charles rose early the following day, eager to begin the tasks that Olivia had handed him. Despite being unflappable, Hunter's face showed surprise at seeing the Duke out of bed so early. After schooling his features, Hunter said, "Breakfast may be a few minutes, your grace. I will tell the cook you are ready to eat."

"Get me a cup of tea, then join me. I have a few tricky tasks to complete today and would welcome your help."

When Hunter poured the tea, Charles dismissed the other footman and said, "Sit, Hunter. I don't want to get a crick in my neck. I am sure I can rely on your discretion in this matter. Last night, the Lady who visited me was Miss Olivia, the second daughter of Edward Clayborne."

The Duke waited for a moment, and Hunter nodded.

"The lady whose father refused to let you court her, even though the lady was agreeable?"

"Yes. Lady Olivier's sister's beau was the impetus that caused Lord Clayborne to refuse my suit. Olivia said she had recently heard snippets of conversation showing Brunswick is trying to convince Lady Georgia to elope with him. He has a nerve, complaining that my association with Olivia would ruin her reputation and her sister's by association, when he intends to ruin Georgia by eloping. The reason for the elopement calls into question the man's integrity."

"What can I do to help, your grace?"

"I need to get a special license from the magistrate this morning and investigate Brunswick. Could you call that nosy friend of yours to help? He can hire as many helpers as he chooses, provided they deliver results. And the faster, the better, as the predicament is dire."

"I can set that in motion, but can I ask about the special license?"

Charles laughed. "I wondered if that registered. Once I give Lord Clayborne the information relating to Brunswick, I will ask the court to see Olivia again. She asked me if her father refused, would I elope with her. I am not driving to the wilds of Scotland for a wedding over the anvil, so that a special license will do."

Hunter grinned. "Well done, my lord. The woman shows pluck, having arrived here in the pitch of night. You organise the license, and I will send a footman to ask Blake to call."

Charles sighed—the easiest part of the tasks he set himself after Olivia's visit was gaining the marriage license. Hunter's friend, Blake, called in contacts around the country to investigate Brunswick. Charles became agitated at the slow progress of the investigation. If Georgia and Brunswick eloped before he could speak to Lord Clayborne, his ability to pressure the man into courting Olivia was lost. No information was forthcoming until they found an associate of Brunswick. The saying, " There's no honour among thieves, " proved true. After a hefty bribe, Brunswick's so-called friend gave the sleuths all they needed to further their investigation. Now Charles had the ammunition to bring Lord Clayborne to heel. The man had better play fair, or Charles intended to use the marriage license to give him the bride he wanted.

Charles called to meet with the earl at the house, but the butler informed him that Lord Clayborne was not receiving visitors. He had the urge to bully his way into the place, but that was not conducive to future cordial relationships.

"Can you give me some paper and a pen? I need to leave a message for Lord Clayborne."

Once he had written the note, Charles waited for a response. The butler returned; his face was expressionless, and his voice a monotone.

"I'm sorry, Lord Clayborne is not receiving."

"Damnation, man, Lady Georgia is in peril. When the scandal reaches society, will you pretend you didn't know? Let me in to talk to the pigheaded man. If he doesn't care for his daughter's safety, I will go to the mother or the daughter."

Grayson dithered for a few moments; having helped Olivia with the carriage and driver, he knew the younger daughter could be in peril, but he would get his marching orders if he defied his master. Olivia walked towards the entrance.

"Grayson, let him in to see Father. My father needs to act immediately on the information the Duke has collected."

"If the earl sacks you for allowing me in, I will hire you."

Grayson stepped back to allow Charles to enter.

"Follow me, your grace."

Charles winked at Olivia and followed the butler.

Charles didn't bother knocking; he pushed the door open without allowing Grayson to announce him.

"What the devil are you doing here? I'll fire that worthless butler. I told him I was not receiving."

"The threat of termination means nothing. I've said I'll hire the man, but do you not care for Lady Georgia?"

"Don't be absurd, man. Of course, I care for my daughter. How dare you?"

"I dare because Lord Brunswick is trying to bully Lady Georgia into eloping with him. Olivia always had reservations regarding the man and asked me to investigate him. The information I collected is horrifying, considering the man is ready to claim your daughter."

"When did you see Olivia?"

"Your other daughter is in danger, and that's all you can ask?"

"I will allow you five minutes; if you haven't made your case by then, I will have the footmen evict you."

"You forget yourself, Clayborne. I am a Duke of the realm, and I'll leave when I see fit. I had a known sleuth, and his associates investigated the Brunswick case. His friend, who took a large bribe, says the man has two derelict entailed estates in the country. The estates have no staff;

not even a caretaker is in residence. Although he has a stipend of ten thousand dollars a year, he is in debt to at least three gaming hells: The Palace, The Paladino and The Jewel. His creditors are pressing him for payment, and his only chance of paying them is through Lady Georgia's dowry. He cannot wait six months for the betrothal and marriage preparations to play out, so he is trying to convince her to elope."

Lord Clayborne rubbed a hand over his chin. "Damnation. It will upset Georgia to learn of this. You say that Olivia asked you to investigate the bounder? Now that you have unearthed this plot, what do you want in repayment?"

"You aren't that obtuse that my repayment isn't obvious. I want Olivia, so you must let me court her unless you want a scandal. We intend to proceed, with or without your permission."

Lord Clayborne remained silent for a few moments. Charles did not trust the man, but he had no choice unless he and Olivia used the marriage license he had gained, thus causing a scandal.

"Well, what say you, Lord Clayborne?"

"You must do something for me before I give you leave to court my daughter. Once I give Brunswick his marching orders, he will become more desperate. So that the man doesn't kidnap her, you will escort Georgia around town. I will inform the women that you're escorting Georgia for her safety. In a week or two, when either Brunswick's creditors catch up with him or he leaves the country, I will permit you to court Olivia."

"Hire bodyguards to keep her safe. My supposed change from one daughter to the next will only cause me more problems in my quest for respectability."

"If you want to court Olivia, those are my terms. If I hire bodyguards, you will not receive my permission to court my daughter."

"And you will let the women know what is happening?"

Edward nodded.

Once Charles left, Clayborne congratulated himself on his clever thinking. If the duke had spoken a few selected words to Olivia, he felt certain her infatuation with the man would die. Clayborne had no fear that the man would become enamoured of Georgia, and he could dispose of the cad without him ruining either of his daughters. Clayborne wasn't, as a rule, a devious man, but when it came to the sons-in-law that he acquired, he needed to be sure that a drunken, gambling father would not disadvantage future generations.

Chapter Twelve

Charles's revealing of Brunswick's nefarious intentions caused an uproar in the household. Lord Clayborne explained it had come to his attention that the man was broke and looking for marriage to a wealthy woman to pay his debts. Olivia felt sad for her sister, but it was better to find out before she committed to the man. Her father had no intention of revealing the source of the information that had come to his attention, which chafed with Olivia. Still, she was optimistic her father would permit Charles to court her.

"In response to this evidence, I have sent Brunswick on his way. Now that Georgia has no beau, Lord Duprais has asked to walk out with her."

Olivia leapt to her feet. "That's not true! We have an understanding."

Lady Clayborne looked distressed.

"You didn't approve that appeal, my lord. You know how Olivia fancies the man?"

"Georgia is the elder daughter. Once she settles, we can find a suitable husband for Olivia."

Olivia glared at her father. "You refused to let Charles court me, so why is he suitable for Georgia? I don't believe he asked to court Georgia. You must have forced him to be with her for some reason. Let me speak to him."

"There is no need to talk to the man; he has made his choice, and I hope you have more pride than to chase after a man who doesn't want you."

Olivia fled from the room, her sobs audible in the sitting room.

When Charles arrived to collect Georgia, two things struck him as unusual: Lady Clayborne gave him a chilly reception, and Lady

Georgia was flirty and coy. He missed Olivia and wished that she were his companion that day.

A week passed, and there was no sign of Brunswick. Charles chaffed at the bit; he had not seen Olivia since this ruse started, and was beyond bored with Georgia. Charles would allow the scam to continue for a few more days, and then he intended to call Lord Clayborne to honour his pledge. However, her father refused Charles' request to speak to Olivia. The excuse was that she was busy with her artwork in the garden and asked him not to disturb her.

Olivia tortured herself by watching as Charles collected Georgia for their next outing. She had ceased eating with the family; listening to Georgia wax lyrical about the Duke was too hard. Her anger at both her sister and her father made for uncomfortable companions. Olivia continued to shun social events; the embarrassment and hurt that Charles had caused her were not something she wished to air in public. The only positive thing from this debacle was her improved relationship with her mother. Maybe her mother's infatuation with another gentleman made her sympathetic to Olivia's suffering, or perhaps she could see the arrangement's unfairness. Olivia was sure that whatever the reason for Charles's supposed change of heart, her father had manipulated the situation, but for what purpose, she was unsure.

With her sketchbook in hand, she wandered the gardens. She found that her mind wandered far too often to allow her to complete a drawing. Sometimes, Olivia started a picture, only for it to develop into a drawing of Charles. He never left her mind, and Olivia wondered if losing the man she loved to her sister would ever not hurt. She might understand his motives if she could talk to him, but was revisiting him in the middle of the night wise? As she wandered, Olivia heard a commotion at the far gate. When she walked towards it to investigate the disturbance, Olivia found herself face-to-face with a large, intimidating man. The intruder wore a face mask, and fear coiled in her stomach. As she turned to flee, the man grabbed her. A cloth covered her nose and mouth, and Olivia remembered no more.

When she woke, Olivia lay still, trying to gauge her predicament. She was in a moving vehicle, and rope bound her hands and legs.

"Well, well, Miss Olivia, you're awake."

Olivia jerked when she recognised the voice.

"You! Why am I here? What is the meaning of this? What are you going to do with me?"

Brunswick grinned. "If I can't get to your sister's dowry, I will get yours. Dumped by your lover, you race into the arms of your sister's former beau, and we marry in Scotland."

"You can't make me marry you. I knew you wore a dishonourable cad, but Charles unearthed your evil plot."

The man laughed. "It didn't do you any good, considering he is courting your sister instead of you."

"My father won't release my dowry to you, even if you force me to marry."

Brunswick sneered at her.

"Of course, he will. When I threaten to leave your beaten and bloody body on the road, the man will run to his bank."

Olivia lay on the floor of the carriage, despair gripping her. Every rut in the road jolted her, and her back ached from the rough ride. The rope chafed her skin, and although she twisted her hands, she couldn't loosen the bindings. Lord Brunswick watched her with amusement.

"I always thought you were feisty, much more interesting than your sister. I would have asked to court you, but I knew you were brighter than that pinhead of a sister and might work out what I planned before I convinced you to elope."

"I would never have welcomed you as a suitor, and nothing you could say would encourage me to elope with you."

"Well, I should have kidnapped you the first night I saw you, but I thought subtlety would be best. Never mind, I end up with the feisty debutant and the dowry. A successful plot, if I do say so myself,"

Despair washed over Olivia. How long would it be before someone realised she was missing? Would Charles care if she had disappeared or continued courting her sister and announcing their marriage while Brunswick carried her further away?"

As the sun began its daily descent, Olivia wondered how long Brunswick intended to travel. The trip seemed endless, and the pain caused by the bumps and jolts of the carriage as she lay on the floor wore her down. The horses must need changing over, and even if Brunswick was comfortable in the carriage, the driver must need a rest? Could she call for help at one of the staging stations or an inn if Brunswick stopped for the night? Olivia comforted herself, hoping her predicament might not be as dire as she suspected. She needed to exercise patience and wait for an opportunity to escape.

When the coach slowed, Olivia's hope soared. Could she try to escape or call the publican for help? Brunswick rose from his seat and grabbed a blanket from the rear of the carriage. He wrapped her in the rug and said, "The publican and his wife will not aid you. They have a hefty bribe in their pockets to ignore whatever goes on tonight. Don't waste your energy."

He pulled her roughly from the carriage and entered the bar. He carried her through the taproom and up the stairs to the accommodation. None of the patrons paid her any heed, and Brunswick made his way, unchecked, to the stairs. Olivia's skin crawled at the sensation of Brunswick's arms around her. Once inside the bedroom, he tossed her on the bed and untied her. Her arms were sore from being tied behind her back, and the rub marks on her ankles stung. As she moved her arms around, pins and needles caused her to groan aloud. Brunswick chuckled.

"Did the carriage not live up to your lofty standards? A maid will bring you food, and you'd best prepare for your wedding night."

"You can't. We're not married."

"We'll just pre-empt the wedding, shall we? I'm sure it's happened a time or two."

Her prospective groom winked at her as he closed the door. Olivia continued to shake the pins and needles in her arms. She searched the room for an escape route, but it seemed unlikely she could escape. The window was not a choice, as it was a two-storey building. Olivia slumped on the bed, and the tears she had fought off all day spilled. The knock on the door and the key turning in the lock froze her to the spot. A maid arrived with food on a tray.

"His lordship said you might want help to remove your dress."

"His lordship is a scoundrel who kidnapped me. I won't remove my dress to make it easier for him to force himself on me. Leave the food and get out. I hope your corrupt boss is happy with the rape and abduction of a maiden lady."

The maid's face paled, but she walked out, locking the door behind her. Noise filtered through the floorboards; the inn was full of patrons. Olivia forced herself to eat; there was no point in starving herself to death. If Brunswick spent a long time with the other patrons, he might become too intoxicated when he returned to force himself on her. Olivia stalked around the room, looking for any potential weapon or way of escape. She had both of the tactics Charles had taught her, but she wasn't sure if she could disable Brunswick long enough to race out the door. Would the publican stop her if she ran through the taproom? With nothing available, she drifted towards the window. Her heart leapt when she realised a ledge was outside the building. The ledge ran the entire length of the building and looked wide enough for her dainty feet.

With no time to spare, she eased the window open. Sliding one leg over the sill, Olivia balanced on the window frame and inched her leg toward the ledge. A wave of fear gripped her as she searched for the ledge with her foot. Was there another alternative to walking along a narrow ledge two storeys above the ground? Trying to overpower Brunswick might work, but the publican who pocketed a large bribe was unlikely to let her walk out the door, so no, there was no alternative. The scariest step was the first; after that, she had no choice but to continue her escape attempt. Olivia carefully edged her way along the ledge. With her back pressed against the building, she took one careful step after another.

The shelf was wide enough for her to place her foot sideways and then replace it with the other. Inching along the ledge, Olivia prayed nobody left the inn and looked up; if that happened, she would be discovered immediately. When her foot slipped, she grabbed wildly at the partially open shutter on the window beside her. The shutter slid towards her, and Olivia feared that she would fall to the ground. Replacing her foot on the ledge, she leaned against the shutter, and it settled back against the window. Olivia took a calming breath and resumed her trek across the shelf. There was no point working her way around to the front of the building. Who knew what lies Brunswick had told the tavern keeper and the patrons? The ledge ended at the roof that led to the stable. Did she dare try to jump from the shelf to the roof? Olivia stayed low and looked at her surroundings. No patrons were walking in this part of the yard, and if she jumped, no one would sound the alarm. If Olivia could access the stable roof, something might help her descend to the ground. She had no choice. If she didn't risk leaping from the rooftop, the alternative was to stay here and marry Brunswick after he compromised her. With a deep breath, Olivia stepped to the edge of the shelf and jumped.

Olivia cringed at the noise she made landing on the stable roof and looked around to see if the patrons had run out to investigate. The sound in the bar remained steady, and no curious eyes scanned the building for the cause of the disturbance. Olivia scurried across the roof. At the farthest side, a barrel of rainwater stood against the wall. She turned so her stomach lay against the tin roof and lowered her legs. When her first foot, and then the second, landed on the rim of the drum, she sighed with relief. One last jump, and she landed on the ground outside the stable. A peek into the stalls revealed no grooms or stable hands still at work. Olivia scanned the horses in the barn. The pair that had pulled their carriage was too tired to make a swift getaway. She hated to steal someone else's property, but she had no choice but to do so. The horse closest to the door was large and resembled a working horse. Could she straddle him, and was he used to being ridden? As she approached the enormous horse, he stretched his head and whickered. "Good boy. You and I are going on a journey."

The working horse stood still while Olive slipped a bridle in place. Once she climbed up the partition, Olivia eased onto the broad back. There wasn't time to find a saddle that fit the carthorse, and without one, she needed to concentrate on staying on the horse's back. She leant forward, unhitched the gate, and nudged the horse into a fast walk. When no one called out after her, she pushed the horse into a canter. The huge horse was willing, but it was bigger than anything Olivia had ever ridden. When she stretched out her horse on their country property, her mount was free and compliant, but even though this horse was cooperative, his gait suggested that he was unaccustomed to being ridden. The journey home would test her endurance, but she was determined to return home.

Chapter Thirteen

As Olivia reached the road, she realised that her task was mammoth. Should she have run to a nearby house and asked for help? The promise of restitution often swayed reluctant helpers, but what if she didn't find a sympathetic woman? Her plight could only worsen if she had encountered a less-than-chivalrous gentleman. No, she was better, only relying on herself. Her way was lit by the moon, for the most part, but when the moon slid behind the clouds, it was almost pitch-black. Olivia tried to focus on the road ahead so that she and he mount didn't end up in a ditch when the moon disappeared.

Olivia listened for another rider, terrified that Brunswick would come after her. Once or twice, the sound of hoofbeats caused her to seek refuge in the trees, but thankfully, the oncoming riders did not see her. Olivia was bone-tired after riding all night. She found it challenging to stay upright on her mount. The horse had walked and cantered each time she asked him, but she knew he must be tiring. The sun peeked through the morning clouds, and she knew she needed a place to lie low during the daylight hours. Although she wanted to return home as soon as possible, riding during the day might put her at risk of being recaptured by Lord Brunswick. The outline of a hay shed was the only building she could see on the horizon. She scrutinised the shed in the distance; it would have to do. Would spending the day there be too obvious if Brunswick came looking for her

Once she reached the hay shed, she scanned the field for a farmhouse or other dwelling. She couldn't see any other home, so she slid off the horse. Her legs buckled as she hit the ground, and she rested for a few seconds before pushing herself back to her feet. Before she slept, she had to attend to the horse. Piles of fresh hay filled the shed. Pulling a mound of the sweet-smelling feed, she led the horse to the back of the shed so that no one could see him from the road. The animal pushed its nose into the feed before eating. Olivia returned to the front of the shed twice more, constructing a pallet on which to sleep. She grasped the end of the horse's reins and fell asleep.

A man's voice roused her, and Olivia sprang up. She backed away from the elderly man, gauging whether she could outrun him. He held both hands up, hoping to appease her.

"I will not hurt you, Miss. But you must admit that a young lady sleeping behind my hayseed is not an everyday occurrence."

"Please, sir, when I get home, I can send money for the hay my mount has eaten."

"Why are you here, unattended, riding a carthorse bareback? Where is home?"

"Ah, it's a lengthy story."

The man rubbed his chin and looked over his shoulder.

"I tell you what. Why don't you let me leg you onto that monstrous horse, and we can go to the farmhouse if you follow me? My wife, Mary, will be excited to have a visitor, and you can tell us your story."

"I don't want to cause any fuss. If you leave me here for the day, I will leave at sundown."

"And when I go home and tell Mary about you, she will scold me. Please accept my offer; we will care for you today."

Olivia followed the farmer as he led her towards a farmhouse set below the rise of the hill. When he explained where he had found Olivia to his wife, the kind woman invited her in. Mary was a cheerful soul who fussed over Olivia as though she were royalty. Once she had a warm bowl of soup, Olivia told the kind strangers her story. The farmer, Henry, expressed his outrage at her poor treatment. Mary patted her hand.

"Why don't you sleep here for the day? Henry can stable the horse, and just before sundown, I will wake you. After you have a bite to eat, you can be on your way."

Tucked up in a warm bed, Olivia remembered the greedy landlord who ignored her plight, and she felt grateful that there were kind people like the couple caring for her. Her last thought before she fell asleep was a prayer that her presence here wouldn't bring trouble to their door.

When Henry led the horse around, Olivia noticed the saddle. The farmer grinned at her.

"I found a saddle to fit him. The saddle will make the ride easier on you and him because you can trot with stirrups. I tell Mary that you should never throw things away; you never know when you might need them. Let me leg you up."

Olivia felt tears well in her eyes. "You and your lady wife are wonderful people. I thank my lucky stars that your hay shed was where I rested. Once I am home, I will return the saddle to you."

"Godspeed, my lady."

Olivia travelled through the night, the trusty horse plodding on relentlessly. The moon, brighter tonight than last night, seemed to light her way home. Her journey was straightforward, and she encountered no fellow travellers. As the sun rose the following day, she rode through the gate of their townhouse. A stable boy strolled out onto the driveway, judging the importance of the visitor by the horse she rode. Without approaching, he sneered at the rider.

"What do you want?" he asked.

Her tolerance ended there.

"I want you to get your lazy self over here to help me dismount, and then I want you to treat this horse as the most valuable piece of horseflesh in the stables. And if you sneer at guests because you disapprove of their transport, maybe you should find employment elsewhere."

The stable boy's jaw dropped, and he raced towards Olivia. He muttered his apologies while helping her to dismount. As her legs gave way, she held onto the stirrup leather, not wanting to take the offered hand of the servant. Once her legs steadied, she said,

"Make no mistake. If I return and find that horse out in a paddock or still sweaty, I will have your hide."

With long strides, Olivia headed for the front door. When Grayson opened the door, he blinked in surprise, and then an enormous grin split his face.

"Miss Olivia, we were so afraid for you. Your father and the Duke have been scouring the countryside for you. Where have you been?"

"I have been touring the countryside, first tied and bound on the floor of Brunswick's carriage and then on the back of a mammoth workhorse. Grayson, please ask the footman to organise a bath for me, and I will be in the kitchen with Mrs Hewson. I need food and a cup of tea, and I will tell you the details of my kidnapping. I need to go to bed, but have my mother or Georgia rouse me when they wake."

After riding hard all day, Lord Clayborne and Lord Duprais still could not find the kidnapped girl. They stopped at the inn where Brunswick had bribed the owners, but couldn't get any answers from the tavern keeper about Olivia's whereabouts. They stayed overnight at the inn and then would continue their search in the morning. Their horses needed a rest, and so did they. They requested their meal in the private parlour, and when the maid delivered their meal, she provided information.

"I'll likely get the sack, but I feel guilty about what happened here. A toff carried a lady in, wrapped in a rug. The toff visited a few days earlier, and he and the master were in the office for a while. As they left the office, I saw money change hands. My master told me to lock the door after delivering the lady her meal. She begged me to help; she said the toff kidnapped her, and he would compromise her and force her to marry him. I didn't know what to do. I decided if I got the swell good and drunk, I might sneak her out later in the dark. But I didn't need to sneak her out of the tavern. A local farmer came in at closing time, raving that someone had stolen his horse. The dandy staggered upstairs; the window was open, and the lady had gone."

"When was this?"

"Ah, two days ago."

"What happened to the toff?"

"He collected his bags and hightailed it out of here."

"Miss, come to Highfields Manor if you want or need employment. I am Lord Duprais, the Duke of Nottingham. I will find a position for you should you need it."

"Thank you, my lord. Can you find a position for me?"

"Yes, we will ride out tomorrow. Be prepared to leave when we do if you're interested in a job. I will put you on the mail coach."

Charles felt buoyed because Olivia had escaped, but the road could be dangerous for an unaccompanied young lady. He yearned to resume his search, but he had to exercise patience and let the horses rest. Tomorrow, they would continue the hunt. There was one thing that gave him hope. If she escaped two days ago, she could well be home already.

The following day, Charles and Lord Clayborne retraced their steps. It seemed impossible to believe that Olivia had escaped and left no trace behind. Had she hidden somewhere and been waiting for someone to find her? The two riders hadn't encountered any houses along the route, so Olivia hadn't taken refuge along the way. As Charles scanned the fields, he noticed a hay shed set well back from the road.

"We haven't seen hide nor hair of Olivia. Mayhap she went to ground somewhere. That hay shed is the only building visible from the road that might offer a hiding place. Let's have a look."

Edward grunted his ascent, and the two trotted across the field.

The hay spread out as a pallet still lay behind the shed, and horse droppings near a pile of hay firmed up their belief that Olivia had taken refuge here. Charles scanned the field. This shed appeared alone, but he knew a house must be nearby. A home appeared once he crossed behind the shed and rode to the other side of the rise. Before the men could reach the house, a farmer in an old tractor spluttered towards them.

"Gentlemen, what brings you to my humble home?"

"We're looking for a woman. It seems she might have rested behind your hay shed. Is that correct?"

The farmer's gaze never shifted. "Who are you, and why are you seeking the woman?"

Lord Edward grunted at Charles. "This stop is a waste of time. Olivia must have rested here without the farmer's knowledge. Let's go."

Charles shook his head. "No. This impatient man is Lord Edward Clayborne, and I'm Lord Duprais. Miss Olivia Clayborne was the victim of a kidnapping. A scoundrel named Brunswick kidnapped her, intending to compromise her and force her to wed. The cad wanted her dowry. We tracked her to the Blue Swallow Inn, and the helpful maid said that Olivia had stolen a horse and escaped. We didn't come across her as we rode out, and the evidence we saw behind the hay shed suggests she rested here. Can you tell us of her whereabouts?"

The farmer's nod was the first sign that someone had seen Olivia after escaping from the inn.

"Why don't you gents come to the house, and I can tell you what happened. If everything went well, Miss Olivia will have arrived home this morning."

As there was no urgency, Lord Clayborne and Charles accepted the man's offer. Over a cup of tea and scones, Mary and Henry recounted what they knew of Olivia's flight to freedom. Lord Clayborne insisted on paying the couple for the care they had taken of his daughter, and then the two gentlemen bid the couple goodbye and headed for home.

The servants bombarded Lord Clayborne and Charles with information about Olivia's kidnapping and escape upon entering the house.

"Grayson, organise food for Lord Duprais and me; we'll take it to the sitting room, and everyone can tell us about what happened. Where is she?"

Lady Clayborne entered the room, accompanied by Georgia. "Olivia has retired for the night. The entire episode wore her out. I believe she will be much better tomorrow."

Lady Clayborne's explanation scuttled Charles's hope of seeing Olivia tonight.

"Might I call on her tomorrow?"

Lord Clayborne looked at Charles, his gaze showing none of his thoughts. With a nod, he said, "Call at morning tea time. You can see her then."

As they ate and chatted, Charles became concerned by the responses he received from the ladies. Lady Clayborne was chilly, and Georgia continued with her flirtatiousness. Confusion clouded Charles' thoughts, and when fatigue caught up with him, he excused himself, stating that he would return to talk to Olivia at morning tea.

Chapter Fourteen

When Charles presented himself at the Saxtons' home, the butler looked confused when Charles asked to see Olivia. "Ah, she left this morning at first light."

Astonishment flicked across the Duke's face, and then rage replaced it. "That lying bastard. Please inform your master that I wish to speak with him. Ask Lady Clayborne and Lady Georgia to join us."

Grayson showed Charles into the sitting room, and soon the ladies joined him. When Lord Clayborne arrived, he demanded,

"What is the meaning of this behaviour? You may be a Duke, but you can't order me around in my house."

"I have demanded that you join your wife and daughter here because I want to show them how little honour you have. I accompanied you on your hunt for Olivia, and while she was resourceful enough to get away herself, your contribution to her welfare was no greater than mine. When I asked to visit her last night, you said I could see her at morning tea, but you intended to send her off early this morning. Isn't that true?"

Lady Clayborne interrupted. "Your grace, you were tireless in hunting for Olivia, but considering you are keeping company with Georgia, why are you so adamant about seeing Olivia?"

Charles looks startled. "What do you mean, keeping company with Georgia?"

Silence fell over the room as the occupants gazed at one another. Charles stood and glared at Lord Clayborne.

"Do you want to tell your woman folk of the deception you have played, or should I do the honours?"

"What rubbish are you prattling, Duprais?" Lord Clayborne blustered.

"Ladies, this man, your husband and father, has played a cruel joke on us. When I uncovered Brunswick's evil intent, I asked to court Olivia as payment, if you will, for saving you, Lady Georgia, from a dreadful marriage. Lord Clayborne told me that if I kept company with Georgia for a few weeks to keep her safe from abduction by Brunswick, I could court Olivia when the danger passed. He promised to tell you why I was with Lady Georgia and that when she was safe, I could court Olivia."

"Edward, how could you do that? You built up Georgia's hopes and broke Olivia's heart. Tell the man where you sent Olivia so he can make this right."

"We have had enough scandals in this family, with Brunswick and a kidnapping. I don't need this bounder to cause more by chasing after my daughter. I will not tell you of Olivier's whereabouts, and that's an end to it."

Lady Georgia glared at her father. "Why set Lord Duprais up to court me if you don't want him as a son-in-law?"

"I didn't think you would entertain his attention for too long, so it didn't concern me."

Charles stalked across the room.

"As a gentleman, your word should be ironclad. How can you now throw out your pact? Did you ever intend to honour our agreement? I did as you asked, even though I had suggested hiring a guard to escort Lady Georgia. You wouldn't have left Olivia vulnerable if you had listened to my suggestion. Tell me where she is. You know I'm not chasing after her. I love her and intend to marry her."

"Grayson, show the Duke out. Get out, Lord Duprais. You may as well not return. I will not divulge my daughter's location."

Charles returned every day for the next week. Every day, Grayson turned him away. Charles could see the regret in the old retainer's eyes, but he would not budge. Hunter tried to keep his master's frame of mind positive, but there was little to encourage the Duke. After thrashing and turning every night for a week, Charles looked exhausted. Where had the man sent Olivia, and why was he so adamant that the couple not marry? When Hunter knocked on his door, Charles had just fallen asleep. Grumbling a reply, he waited to find out what was so crucial for Hunter to interrupt his attempts to sleep.

"My Lord, a lady is downstairs, wishing to speak to you. It is not the same lady who called before, but the carriage is the same."

Charles bounded out of bed. After pulling a shirt on, he waited as Hunter buttoned it and helped him into a jacket.

The Lady who waited for him was Lady Clayborne. Like her daughter, the Lady had worn a disguise. Her arrival stunned Charles.

"My lady, what brings you to my door so late at night?"

"My conscience brings me here, your grace. My husband has treated you poorly, and the predicament has become dire because he intends to sign a marriage contract with Lord Collingwood for Olivia's hand."

Charles's curses were unsuitable for a lady's hearing, but Lady Clayborne forgave him because she felt the same.

"Olivia loathes the man; why would her father do that to her?"

"Because Lord Collingwood threatened to spill the secret of Olivia's abduction and ruin her reputation; also, there was a large sum of money for Edward if he signed the contract."

"What can I do to stop the travesty?"

"You can get a special licence, take this letter for Olivia and ride like the devil to the late Duke's estate at Cotswold. If you are fast enough, you could marry Olivia before we all arrive for her marriage to Collingwood. This instruction may be indelicate, but your grace consummated the marriage immediately, so there can be no hope of an annulment."

Hunter showed Lady Clayborne out and helped her into her carriage. When he re-entered the room Charles was in, he asked,

"Can I help, my lord?"

"That was Lady Clayborne. Lord Clayborne is negotiating a marriage contract for Olivia with Lord Collingwood. I offered for her, and the bastard refused me. Lord Collingwood is a loathsome fellow, and I know Olivia would prefer to become a nun than accept his advances for the rest of her life. If I move fast, I can beat their carriage and marry her before he can stop us. I need to leave just before dawn. Can you ask my valet to pack a small travelling bag? I will ride, not take the carriage, because I need to be fast."

"Your grace, may I offer my best wishes for a speedy trip and a wedding at the journey's end?"

Any hope Charles had of falling asleep disappeared as he thought of the journey ahead. If his sleep had been disturbed since Olivia's disappearance, tonight, as he prepared to rescue Olivia from marriage to a degenerate, sleep was non-existent.

Thank heavens Lady Claybourne had arrived to inform him of Olivia's location; the alternative didn't bear thinking about. Charles never thought he would need to use the special license, but he was thankful that he had heeded Olivia's request to secure the document some weeks ago.

Lord Claybourne's deceit nagged at Charles. The man had lied at every turn, and Olivia's abduction was down to her Father. If the man had hired bodyguards for Georgia, then Olivia would have been protected by his presence. To allow Georgia to think that Charles was interested in her without telling the women the truth was despicable. He knew he had tarnished his reputation after years of drinking, gambling and whoring, but surely his behaviour leading up to his request to court Olivia counted for something? He prayed that when he reached the estate, Olivia would let him explain what was happening; otherwise, she would be married to Collingwood.

Chapter Fifteen

Charles left his townhouse as the sun rose the following day. He pushed hard, hoping his mount had the stamina to reach the Cotswold estate without a rest. The landscape was unfamiliar, and as he navigated the poor roads and tracks, Charles cursed aloud at the fickleness of Olivia's father. As the day wore on, Charles became increasingly agitated; he should have left the previous night, even though riding at night presented challenges. What if he arrived too late to save Olivia from Collingwood's clutches? The idea of Olivia married to Collingwood didn't bear thinking about. Without her mother's intervention, Olivia would be caught unawares when Collinwood presented himself with the marriage contract, and the news that they were to marry would devastate her.

Charles caught sight of a large manor house as his exhausted horse topped a rise. There was no sign of a carriage, and Charles breathed a sigh of relief as he pushed his horse to complete the journey.

A stable hand ran towards him as Charles stopped at the front door.

"Hitch up the carriage and saddle a fresh horse for me and a mount for Miss Olivia. And be quick. I will return in a few minutes and expect them to be ready. Leave my horse to blow while you ready the others."

The boy scuttled off, and Charles headed for the door. The butler opened the door at his approach.

"My Lord, what can I do for you?"

"What's your name, my good man?"

"I'm Benson, my lord."

"Benson, I am Charles Duprais, the Duke of Nottingham, and I will soon be Lady Olivia's husband. Can you tell me where Miss Olivia is? It would be best if you also located the housekeeper. I want you in the carriage out the front as soon as you find her. The reverend expects you. Instruct the driver to go to the village church and make haste. Olivia and I will be there as quickly as possible. Is all that understood?"

"Yes, my lord. Miss Olivia is in the sitting room. I will fetch Mrs Butler."

Charles raced towards the sitting room. Olivia jumped from her seat as the door flew open. The look of astonishment would have amused Charles if her predicament weren't so dire.

"My love, it took me a week to find where they sent you. You need many explanations, but most importantly, your father has negotiated a marriage contract for you with Lord Collingwood."

Olivia's face paled, and she sank into the chair behind her.

"Your mother wrote you a letter, but we must be quick. I don't want to rush you, but time is of the essence. Will you marry me? I got a marriage license a while ago when you suggested we elope, and I spoke to the minister on my way here. Mrs Butler and Benson are going to the church to act as witnesses. Your mother said they were setting out last night so that they will be close."

"Where is the letter?"

Charles pulled the letter from his coat pocket and handed it to her. The note was brief and to the point. Olivia nodded.

"Let's get married, but when we are married, I want explanations. I never thought my wedding would be in a country church with two servants as witnesses."

After Charles helped her mount, the two riders cantered towards the village church. The wedding vows took little time, and the witnesses signed the paperwork. Charles was aware that signing the marriage documents was only half of the job,

"Follow at your leisure, Benson. My Lady and I need to do one more thing to ensure that Lord Clayborne can't annul the marriage. If Lord and Lady Clayborne arrive before we come downstairs, try to stall them. Offer refreshments and whatever else you can do to give me time."

Benson grinned. "As you wish, my lord."

Charles cantered off, and Olivia followed.

"Why are we in a hurry? We are married, so they can't force me to wed that toad."

"Sweetheart, your father can ask the magistrate to annul your wedding unless we consummate the marriage."

Olivia's blush covered her face and neck, and Charles grimaced.

They cantered the horses towards the Manor house and dismounted at the door once they reached their destination. Charles threw the reins at the stable boy and grabbed Olivia by the arm. The servant who opened the door was stunned as the Duke and his new duchess ran past him.

"If anyone arrives before we come downstairs, stall them."

The red-faced servant nodded his agreement.

As they ascended the stairs, Charles felt a stab of regret.

"I have one regret and one apology before getting to your room. I wanted to take it slowly the first time because it can be uncomfortable for the woman. But I fear we don't have time. I ask that you trust me to do this as fast as possible, and then we have a lifetime to enjoy each other."

"Very well, but understand that when the, ah, you know, finishes, you must explain what is happening."

As Charles and Olivia entered her bedroom, the banging on the front door was audible. Charles flipped Olivia onto the bed.

"I'm sorry, sweetheart."

When Charles completed the coupling, he brushed her hair from her face and wiped the tears from her cheeks with his thumb. Her silent tears tore at his heart. But Clayborne had every right to cancel the marriage without this hasty coupling.

"Whatever happens next, please believe that I love you."

Olivia snuggled against her husband.

"I want to stay here, but we had better face the music."

Before they could leave the room, Benson knocked on the door. "My Lady, your father wants you to join the others in the parlour."

Charles opened the door and grinned at Benson.

"I believe we are ready."

Benson smothered his grin. "Very good, my Lord."

"Are you nervous, sweetheart?"

"Yes, my father will not enjoy being defied. I assume there will be lots of shouting and swearing, but Father could have avoided trouble if he had played fair."

"There are many things that your father needs to explain to you. He deceived you, your mother, and your sister and lied to me. Don't feel too sorry for the blighter until you hear of his deceptions."

Charles held out his hand, and Olivia placed her hand in his. He squeezed her hand, and they descended the stairs to face the uproar they knew would ensue.

Benson opened the door, and the couple entered the parlour. Seeing them together and holding hands galvanised Lord Clayborne and Lord Collingwood. Collingwood was all but frothing at the mouth, spittle spraying out as he shouted,

"Get your filthy hands off my fiancé. Olivia, come here to me now. I will not tolerate disobedience from my betrothed."

Olivia shook her head. "Then I extend my sympathy to your betrothed, whoever she may be. I am comfortable standing here next to my husband."

Both men shared the same appalled expression. Lord Collingwood was beetroot red in the face, and her father's paler complexion was worrying. Charles walked with Olivia to a seat near her sister and her mother.

"Gentlemen, we were married a few hours ago. Whatever plans you made for your daughter, Clayborne, we ruined. How could you marry her to a man she loathes? You love your daughter so much that you lied and sold her to this lecher for financial gain? As you didn't tell your wife and Lady Georgia of your duplicity, will you tell Olivia, or will I?"

Lord Collingwood approached Olivia. "I care nothing for lies and truths. If we annul the marriage, we can fulfil the marriage agreement."

Olivia smirked at Collingwood. "I know it's possible to cancel a marriage if the groom doesn't bed the bride. You're too late; we consummated the marriage before you arrived."

Lord Collingwood raged around the room, screaming and yelling, threatening to expose Olivia's kidnapping to the ton. He sneered at Charles. "If she is with child, the ton will wonder if the child is yours or Brunswick's."

"I care not what the ton think. What matters is that I know any child Olivia has is mine. You will see proof if you want to check the bed linen."

Lady Clayborne stood. "Edward, Lord Collingwood, your behaviour is unacceptable. You have behaved dreadfully, and your conduct in this room is equal to that of a toddler's tantrum. If you cannot contain yourselves, I suggest you leave the room until you gain control of yourselves."

Olivia grinned. She had never heard her mother take her father to task, and now she had called him to order and silenced Collingwood. Lady Georgia spoke for the first time.

"Let me congratulate you, Olivia and Lord Duprais, on your marriage. Let us ask Benson for refreshments."

As Georgia walked to the door to call the butler, Lord Collingwood grabbed her and pulled her into his arms.

"If I can't marry the other one, this chit will do."

The room erupted in uproar. Charles was the first person to reach Georgia.

"Get your hands off my sister-in-law, or I won't challenge you to a duel; I'll kill you now."

When Collingwood inched to the door, still holding Georgia, Olivia ducked behind him and fled into the hallway. Benson appeared, and she instructed him to bar the entrance and find a footman to help stop Collingwood from abducting Georgia. The parlour door burst open, and Collingwood backed out, a struggling Georgia in his arms. The man had his back to the hallway, unaware of those who stood behind him. Olivia scanned the entrance, and her eyes spotted a vase that would make a useful weapon. She grabbed the vessel in both hands and brought her makeshift weapon down on Collingwood's head. The man dropped like a stone, releasing Georgia as he plummeted to the ground. For a moment, Olivia thought her sister might swoon, but then she rallied. Georgia's body shook, the tight hold on her emotions when Collingwood grabbed her unravelled. Both women rushed to comfort Georgia; the men focused on trussing up the unsteady nobleman.

Charles took control of the situation as Lady Clayborne and Olivia comforted Georgia.

"Benson, send a man to the magistrate. The rest of you can go back to your jobs. Mrs Butler, can you send a maid to clean up the mess? We will move to the sitting room and would appreciate it if you could send us refreshments."

The housekeeper nodded and rushed towards the kitchen. She needed to locate a maid and inform the cook that the day was far from finished. Charles moved towards his wife and pulled her into his arms. He felt the tension ease as her head rested on his chest.

"Why would the man go to such lengths to find a bride? He must be mad." Olivia shuddered at the memory of Collingwood's threats, and Charles placed his hand on her back and stroked it.

"Get your hands off my daughter, you cad. This fiasco is all your fault." Lord Clayborne grasped Olivia's arm to move her from Charles's embrace. She swung around, wrenching her arm from her father's grasp.

"This mess is all thanks to you, or so I'm told. I am no longer your responsibility; you have no right to tell me what to do. I'm not sure yet what happened with Charles spending time with Georgia, but we would not have needed to resort to deceit if you had let Charles court me. Let us move to the sitting room; I am eager to hear why this fiasco exists."

Once seated in the sitting room, Lady Clayborne asked, "Shall I explain what happened, or do you wish to do so, your grace?"

Charles inclined his head. "Why don't you start, and I'll fill in the spaces?"

"Olivia, this began when your father bowed to Brunswick's demand to send you packing. Something prompted you to ask for assistance from his grace. Lord Duprais set some men to investigate, and when he found Brunswick was a threat to Georgia, he took the information to your father."

Georgia interrupted. "What encouraged you to ask Charles for help, and how did you contact him, because he was always with me?"

"I never trusted that snake Brunswick, and he was always disrespectful. I caught the end of a few private conversations and realised he was trying to convince you to elope. You may have been with Charles every day, but not every night. I hired a driver and a plain conveyance, wearing a disguise, and I visited him one night to ask for his help."

Lord Clayborne let out an enraged shout. "That's why I refused his request to court you, Olivia. If someone had caught you, it would have ruined you."

"If she hadn't taken the risk, Miss Georgia might be lying dead at Brunswick's derelict house. If someone had discovered Olivia, I would have wed her. Do you want to continue, Lady Clayborne?"

"Thank you. So unbeknownst to us, your father insisted Lord Duprais escort Georgia to social events to discourage Brunswick from trying to kidnap her. The agreement was that your father would explain what was happening, and in a few weeks, when the danger had lessened, Lord Duprais could court Olivia."

Charles interrupted. "But the bounder didn't inform you, ladies, and caused hurt and failed expectations. His refusal to employ bodyguards for Georgia placed Olivia in danger."

Olivia glared at her father. "You signed a marriage contract for me with that loathsome man. Why?"

Lord Clayborne sighed. "Because I sent you away, the kidnapping story spread like wildfire. Collingwood came to me and said that unless I signed a marriage contract for you, he would spread the tale that Brunswick compromised both of you girls, and he would tell the ton that the reason I sent you away was that you were with child. And I realised that by refusing Charles's request, I had no option but to comply with Collingwood's demands."

While the men spoke with the magistrate and arranged for Collingwood's removal from the house, the ladies sat in Lady Clayborne's private rooms and discussed the events that had brought them to this point. Olivia needed to talk to her sister about Charles keeping company with her.

"Georgia, I hope that father's ruse has not left you with a broken heart. I know how charming Charles can be, and I don't want any awkwardness between us."

Georgia looked at her hands and lifted her face with a rueful grin.

"I admit your Duke attracted me, and I am disappointed that all was not as I thought. But I learned something from the experience. I learned the qualities I should look for in a suitor and not allow money or titles to influence me. You didn't marry Charles for his wealth or his title, and I shall follow your lead. When Lord Brunswick asked to court me, I felt flattered but never considered that I had to live with the man for the rest of my life."

Olivia grimaced. "From what Charles discovered, the rest of your life would be short. Brunswick intended to kill you and marry another debutant with a healthy dowry. And contrary to Mother's belief, a title does not make a man a gentleman."

Lady Claybourne gave a shamefaced look at her daughters.

"When I married, the money and the title were more important to my parents than the man's character. I was lucky, but others were married to men they hated or men who weren't interested in them, just their dowries. I should have learned from my cohorts' disastrous marriages, but I was still convinced that a title was necessary when we started the season. I'm sorry, I've learned my lesson. Your Duke, Olivia, may have a chequered past, but it's obvious he loves you, and you love him. Your Father was wrong to keep you apart, and his lies make me angry. Forgiving him will take much time, and I don't doubt it will take you even longer."

"Charles told me you had a clandestine meeting with him to tell him where I was and what was happening. Thank you for that; without Charles having that marriage licence, I would be married to that loathsome man."

Georgia giggled.

"Just imagine you two wearing disguises and having late-night meetings with a gentleman. Who knew all that activity was happening after dark?"

Epilogue

Dinner was an awkward meal. The magistrate had removed Collingwood, but the pall of the ruse clung to the occupants in the dining room. Lady Clayborne was still furious at her husband, and the attempted kidnapping had left Georgia pensive. Charles chaffed at the bit; he had no wish to socialise with Olivia's family tonight. Tonight was his wedding night, and he wanted to make amends for the crude coupling that Olivia had endured earlier.

Lady Clayborne hosted the meal, but when the time came for the men to enjoy a drink and a smoke, she released Olivia and Charles.

"Charles, I doubt you want to socialise on your wedding night. When I gave you Olivia's location, I gave you my blessing. Start your life together."

As they left the room, they could hear the angry voice of Lord Clayborne upon discovering that his wife had ruined his plans. Olivia would struggle to forgive her father for nearly ruining her life. The thought of living under Collingwood's rules and submitting to his advances made Olivia feel ill. Lord Clayborne's betrayal would take a long time to forgive, and even time was unlikely to have the matter forgotten.

Charles closed and locked the bedroom door. He followed his wife into the room and stopped her just before she reached the bed.

"Sweetheart, all your father put us through only strengthened my resolve to marry you. Marriage mamas hounded me at the start of the season, and then, as the rumours circulated, they kept their daughters from meeting me. But all the debutants paled into insignificance the day I met you. Never have I enjoyed supper at one of those dratted balls before my time with you. I'm sorry for the hurt your father inflicted, and grateful that you didn't question my instructions on the need to marry in haste."

Olivia placed her hands on Charles's face and kissed him.

"I watched you with Georgia and couldn't reconcile the man I knew to the cad my father described. There is a positive from your time with my sister; she says she will not allow another man to court her until she has feelings for him. Her inexperience allowed Brunswick to dupe her, but she is wiser now, and other men will have to step up to the mark before she considers their propositions."

Charles nodded. He liked Georgia but found her lack of maturity and naivete trying. He hoped this debacle would help her mature before accepting another man. But it wasn't Georgia who should occupy his mind. He pushed all thoughts aside and focused on his wife.

"I regret bedding you in such a crude fashion, so now I intend to make love to my wife. Do you have any objections?"

Olivia grinned at her husband. "I'm game if you are."

She squealed when Charles grabbed her and threw her on the bed. With memories of their first rough coupling, "Minx" was all he said as he progressed to show her how much better he could do.

Also by Robyn C Rye

Farnsworth Sisters
Marrying a Rogue
Rescuing Hannah

The Buckingham Sisters
Lady Maggie's Challenge
Layla's Unwanted Husband

The Evans Family
Sometimes Love is not Enough
Still the One
Moving Forward

Standalone
One More Chance
Lady Jayne's Reputation
Third Time's the Charm
Can't Stop Loving You

The Marriage Scam
An Unlikely Match
Searching For You
The Unexpected Suitor
The Lady and the Duke
Starting Over
An Unforgettable Stranger
The Duke's Revenge
The Temporary Wife
Against The Odds
Betrayed
No Good Turn Goes Unpunished
Lady Eloise's Soldier
Lillian's Forbidden Beau
Remember Me
Always Second Best
When One Door Closes
Coming Home to You
Chasing Shadows
Fool Me Once
Deserting Lady Audrey
My Unlikely Saviour
Lies and Deception
A New Beginning
Julia's Second Chance
The Hidden Enemy
The Maiden's Redemption
Miss Elizabeth's Season

www.ingramcontent.com/pod-product-compliance
Lightning Source LLC
Chambersburg PA
CBHW050546160726
48003CB00002B/785